what remains after a fire

PRAISE FOR *WHAT REMAINS AFTER A FIRE*

'*What Remains After a Fire* is a visceral and melancholic collection, surrendering to that liminal space of exile—both physical and emotional. With prose [that is] taut yet evocative, Kanza Javed pulls at the seams of her labyrinthine characters, often revealing the dark interiors of the human heart. These stories will stay with me for a long time.'

—**Aanchal Malhotra**, author of *Remnants of a Separation* and *The Book of Everlasting Things*

'*What Remains After a Fire* is a rich, impelling story collection. Kanza Javed's skill as a storyteller, her use of a quiet, nuanced narrative to create the emotional complexities of her characters, and [her] vivid descriptions of their lives—ranging from social pressures and inequalities of gender and/or class to coping with inner conflicts or adjusting to alien lands—add to the book's originality and significance.'

—**Muneeza Shamsie**, editor of *In the New Century: An Anthology of Pakistani Literature in English*

'*What Remains After a Fire* blazes with righteous indignation at the plight of its varied characters: victims of poverty, superstition, prejudice and religious traditions in both Pakistan and America. With an unflinching but compassionate gaze, Javed crafts stories that are disturbing and heartbreaking. A wonderful [short story] debut that establishes Javed as a writer to watch.'

—**Thrity Umrigar**, author of *The Space Between Us* and *Honor*

'Vivid and mesmerizing, this is a collection filled with beautifully wrought stories and characters who will stay with you long after you finish. Javed reveals the loss and longing of layered lives with gorgeous prose and acute observations about the human condition. A magnificent [short story] debut that is powerful and deeply moving.'

—**Marjan Kamali**, author of *The Lion Women of Tehran*

what remains after a fire

KANZA JAVED

Harper Collins

First published in the United States of America by
W.W. Norton & Company
This edition published in India by HarperCollins *Publishers* 2025
HarperCollins *Publishers* India, Cyber City,
Building 10-A, Gurugram, Haryana – 122002, India
www.harpercollins.co.in

2 4 6 8 10 9 7 5 3 1

P-ISBN: 978-93-6213-273-4
E-ISBN: 978-93-6213-593-3

Typeset in 11.5/15.7 Sabon LT Std
by HarperCollins *Publishers* India Pvt. Ltd

Printed and bound at
Thomson Press (India) Ltd

MIX
Paper | Supporting responsible forestry
FSC® C010615

This book is produced from independently certified FSC® paper
to ensure responsible forest management.

HarperCollins *Publishers*, Macken House, 39/40 Mayor Street Upper,
Dublin 1, D01 C9W8, Ireland

For the unmoored, tethered to places that refuse to claim them.

At the end of my suffering
there was a door

—Louise Glück, 'The Wild Iris'

Contents

Rani

My grandmother kept calling her dead husband to bed. On the night of the funeral, Daddi looked for my grandfather in the folds of her velvet blanket, the hollows of her cheeks, and the flickering flames in the gas heater. She sang ballads as if Dadda was lost somewhere: forgotten in a forest, interwoven in the fabric, burning in the fire, braided into the silver of her hair.

The family had just buried him that morning, and Daddi did not remember anything about the ordeal.

No one in the village of Bismillahpur expected my grandfather to live for as long as he did. He had survived the 1947 partition, the 1965 war, a bankruptcy, and two heart attacks. He was eighty-nine when he died, his frail body finally surrendering to heart attack number three. After the second, my parents and I had begun to believe that he had achieved some kind of immortality. He had cheated God.

He was enshrouded in a cloak of invincibility. Dadda was to remain forever.

The news of the death rattled everyone but Daddi. She slept next to his dead body for two nights, until a maid returning from her weekend off discovered them. She called my parents in Lahore. It was a three-hour drive to the village. I drove while my parents sobbed.

I had just moved back into the family house after my divorce. My decision to end my five-year marriage had hit my parents hard, fracturing something deep inside them. They believed that marriages, no matter how bad, no matter how cursed, should not die an early, unnatural death. They should be endured. Pushed through. Dealt with.

When Dadda died, they snivelled and sniffled in their seats. Some things in life are inevitable, like the death of an old man who had already outlived all his siblings and cousins. It was a natural thing to have happened. The time had come. But to leave a husband who was still living and walk out of my in-laws' house, childless and penniless, was an unnatural thing. I had committed a terrible crime.

The weight of the hasty funeral fell on my shoulders. My father removed himself from the task, as he was mourning something else—both his sons, my older brothers, had remained in Michigan and offered condolences over the telephone. They could not make travel arrangements on such short notice. So the village of Bismillahpur watched a thirty-four-year-old divorced woman orchestrate her dead grandfather's funeral: order clean white linen to wrap the body in and arrange for the funeral prayers.

Summon men to bathe the body and dig the grave. Remind mourners that the widow had Alzheimer's and could not utter anything with certainty except the words '*Accha, accha.*'

Yes, yes.

I drew the heavy curtains in the bedroom so the light could meet my grandmother's aging, grey eyes. She sat up from her charpoy and looked at the sunlight filtering through the barred window. The light illuminated only her neck and baby blue sweater—the rest of her body remained immersed in shadows. She sat there for a moment, hollowed out.

Two weeks had passed since the burial. My parents returned to Lahore so that my father could resume his work as an assistant professor of economics at Government College. I was told to stay back for another two weeks in Bismillahpur and pack Daddi's belongings, clean and lock the house, pay the servants their fair dues, and oversee the work being done by the farmers who worked on my grandparents' farmlands. Wheat, peas and cabbage had to be sown. Rice had already been harvested. I did not volunteer for this. My mother believed that since my divorce, I had too much idle time on my hands. I did not have a husband to cook for or a baby to nurse or a job to go to. I did nothing but sit in the winter sunshine of our Lahore home and read books. I refused to meet new men or atone for the sin of losing a husband by grieving and praying before God. When relatives came to inquire about what had happened in my marriage, I retreated to my room and stayed there. No woman in the family had ever gotten a divorce before. Since there was no redemption in my new, disgraceful, unrepentant way of living, I was tasked with packing up Daddi's life so she could move into our house in Lahore.

I did not mind my punishment. I did not mind being shameless. I did not mourn for anything. Not my punishment. Not my failed marriage. And not my dead grandfather. As I was turning off the heater in the bedroom, Daddi flung out her foot from the blanket and dangled it in the air. She sat there for a while, her eyes vacant. I gently took her arm and walked her out of the bedroom to the bathroom.

I sat on a small plastic stool and waited for her to finish. As she was sitting on the white commode, she mumbled something about Sakina, the maid. I told her she was making us breakfast.

Daddi said she wanted dinner.

I said Sakina was making us dinner, then.

I washed her with a Muslim shower and lifted her from the commode, only to realize that the excrement had trickled down her leg, staining her off-white shalwar. I filled two buckets with hot water, warmed the freezing bathroom with an electric heater, and removed Daddi's dirty clothes

In the weeks following the funeral, we developed a simple, everyday routine. It fell into predictable patterns. After breakfast, Daddi, Sakina, and I sat in the sunny courtyard. Sakina chopped vegetables and cleaned rice and lentils for lunch. I read the Urdu newspaper and stories from women's magazines out loud to the ladies. I do not know if Daddi understood what I read, but she nodded as I exaggerated the dialogue.

'*Accha, accha,*' she said.

I told myself that she was following along.

On days when Daddi remembered knitting, she knitted. On days when she remembered that I was Quratulain, Annie, her granddaughter, she massaged my scalp with almond or mustard oil. Our excitement arrived in the form of guests who stopped by for a cup of chai and gossip. It was usually a prying neighbour or a farmer offering condolences. Since Daddi was not the same, such visits were rare. Shabana, the next-door neighbour, remained a faithful guest. Once, she brought her six-year-old daughter Fatimah with her. As Fatimah dunked a Gala biscuit in her mother's chai, Daddi called her for a massage: 'Come here, Annie. Come here, little Annie.' Fatimah looked at me, confused, and I gently reminded Daddi that I was Annie, not the six-year-old. Daddi looked confused but tried to hide it.

The only thing that really varied in our routine was Sakina's selection of lentils and vegetables, my choice of story, or Daddi's mind. After Daddi retired for her afternoon nap, I took on the important things. With Sakina's help, I slowly packed my grandparent's clothes in suitcases and trunks. I took down the curtains from the drawing and dining rooms; discarded unwanted items; called my friend in Lahore and spoke of small, inconsequential things that wove through our days. Her new hair colour. Her complacent father-in-law. Her forgetful mother-in-law. An orange stray cat who stole a leg piece from the kitchen counter. I took long baths and rubbed the sticky mustard oil out of my hair, watching as it washed down the drain.

One night as Sakina was preparing to head back home after serving dinner, Daddi sprang out of her bed and began dressing in front of the mirror. She said she was getting ready for her wedding to Ghulam Awais—Dadda.

For a while, Sakina and I did not interfere, but instead let Daddi play, let her entertain the delusion. We watched her apply black kohl under her eyes and braid a green and gold parranda into her hair. Her fingers, weathered and skilled, deftly twisted the golden threads. We had gotten used to her vague ramblings, the paranoia, the hallucinations and memory jumps. It was a sad disease, but it was a disease. It had to be dealt with kindly.

Daddi existed in fragments, in vapours. I was unable to fully capture her in those weeks as I could when I was a child: crawling into her lap, fitting my little body in her arms, running my fingers through her wet hair after she bathed. The old Daddi carried the smell of red Lifebuoy soap, sharp and antiseptic, and almond hair oil, sweet and nutty. Her fingernails were always stained umber from henna. I knew that when she was smiling and looking down at me, she was looking down only at me. She could see nothing and no one else in the world. She was only mine.

The new Daddi spoke tirelessly to her dead mother on the telephone. She sang to the swirling flames in the fire. She scolded the news anchor on television, told me I was poisoning her tea. And she referred to Sakina as 'Rani'. Rani. I hated hearing that name. It upset me. I ignored Daddi whenever she said it.

The three of us were sitting together in Daddi's room. Sakina chuckled as Daddi draped a shawl around her head and became a bride. Suddenly, her chuckling pained me. 'Get out of the room! Go back home!' I cried, prompting the young maid to leap out of her chair and run out the door. That night as I removed the shawl from Daddi's head and prepared her for bed, she beckoned me closer and whispered, 'Annie, Annie, where is the baby?'

Silence fell as I looked down at her dismayed face. There were black kohl specks on her wrinkled cheek. I dipped the corner of my shawl in a glass of water on her end table and gently erased the stains.

If Daddi had uttered the name 'Rani' in front of my parents or Shabana or Sakina, they would have laughed it off, marked it as one of her many hallucinations. But I knew who she was remembering. I turned off the lights in the bedroom and lulled my grandmother to sleep with a 'Shhh … Shhh …'

Daddi did not lull, though. All through the night, she kept asking for the baby.

✦

The next afternoon, our routine continued as normal, for the most part. Shabana was visiting again, sipping chai and stitching a loose button on one of my sweaters. Sakina sat on a stool near us and kneaded dough for the rotis. But Daddi asked again for Rani, would not stop asking, her haunting chant reverberating in my thoughts.

'Who is this Rani?' asked Shabana, looking at me. 'I don't know,' I lied, and waved off the question. 'Was it a maid? Is it a cousin?'

'I don't know,' I echoed, and urged Sakina to quickly make a roti for the yellow lentils she had prepared.

I watched Shabana's long fingers, chipped with red nail polish, move up and down with the thread and the needle, and as I did, an old memory began to unspool in my mind. Daddi was not always like this. Haggard. Strewn and scattered, like a tree in a storm. Like a fire dying in the hearth. She had been a magnificent woman. Grand. Vital to the family.

Sakina stopped kneading and stood up. She straightened the back of her long kameez and then stooped to lift the steel dish with the dough.

'You know, Quratulain baji,' she said, 'Daddi told me months ago that she saw a woman coming down the stairs from the barsati.'

I looked at the stairs that led to the barsati, the room on the roof.

'She said the woman had blood on her shalwar,' Sakina laughed.

'Bakwas,' I said. 'That's rubbish.' Sakina shrugged.

Shabana brought the thread to her mouth and snapped it with her teeth. The loose button was fixed.

'When my grandfather began to lose his memory,' she said, 'he started seeing strange things, too. He said the trees in the village were walking. His house spoke to him all night. My mother used to say that a witch put a curse on him when he was a boy for torturing all the cats and dogs in the village. It was a punishment for his crime.'

'That's rubbish,' I repeated.

'I don't know, Annie Baji, but this is what my mother told me.' Shabana stood up and handed me the sweater. 'She said we lose our minds because of the bad things we do. They never leave us.'

Every bone, every pulsing vein in my body wanted to reject Shabana's words about a curse. But I was unable to, because I remembered. I could remember everything from my childhood clearly, could remember that time when I lived with my grandparents.

All my adult years, the memories came to me in waves. I had tried to push them away, to make sure they stayed distant, like the cold water of the ocean that bubbles and foams on the shore but never touches your toes. You fear the tides from a distance, careful not to let them sweep you away. But you cannot stop them.

✦

I was nine. May had just begun.

My father had received a scholarship to complete a PhD at the University of Massachusetts in Amherst. My mother went along to help him settle down in an apartment. It was a big move for my parents. Before this, they had never left the country, never lived without a kitchen maid, never lived in a small one-bedroom apartment.

My brothers were sent to stay with an uncle in Karachi who had two boys their age, and I was sent to my grandparents in the village.

I slowly grew used to my grandparents and their behaviours. Daddi would roam around the big house with a bunch of keys she kept stored in her bra. She asked after all the servants: if the watchman had done his duties that night; if the stable boys had fed the cows, hens and donkey; if the maids had cleaned all the bedrooms and bathrooms. She scheduled her weekly meetings with the farmers and the neighbours. Her shrill, commanding voice and booming laughter echoed in the corridors.

Daddi marched here and there, in the open courtyard and in the shadows. Dadda, on the other hand, handled the external affairs: the tenants, the rent, the sowing, harvesting, and selling of wheat, rice and maize.

In the evenings, we sat in the cool courtyard and had tea. The servants' shifts changed at that hour. A watchman named Iftikhar arrived for duty, and a maid named Nargis prepared our dinner and beds.

My grandparents had just hired Nargis. She was a young woman, divorced twice. She had been married first at fourteen to a cousin, and then, after he left her, to a cleric with two wives and six daughters. He wanted a son, but she gave him nothing. Nargis was labeled as barren, a cursed woman whose husbands did not want her, and whose family would not accept her back. Dadda had found her wandering through the village one afternoon, knocking at the doors of the big brick houses, asking for a job as a maid.

So Nargis became a tenant in my grandparents' barsati. They cut the rent of the upstairs room from her salary. In the mornings, when I was doing my summer homework in the courtyard downstairs, I could see her strolling up on the balcony. She watched over the red chillies left to dry in the sun, the blankets and clothes spread out on different charpoys to kill the musty trunk odour. She cleaned the lentils and the rice for lunch. She fed the animals and massaged Daddi's legs with different oils.

Nargis was always sweet to me. She called me guriya, a doll. '*Guriya, guriya.*' She pinched my cheeks when she found me scuttling around the house, playing with Daddi's kohl and rouge. In the afternoons, when my grandparents retired for their naps, I snuck up to the barsati with my Barbie to spend time with Nargis.

Nargis played songs on her radio and combed the doll's hair, styling it differently each afternoon. Her fingers worked through Barbie's glistening golden locks. She remarked on the texture and the light colour of the doll's hair, how she wished she had hair like that, seemingly unaware of her own—beautiful, thick and black.

I had never seen hair like hers. Hair that spoke to the breeze. Hair that had conversations with monsoons. I had a bowl cut, my mother had blonde streaks in her frizzy brown hair, and my grandmother's head was stained mud-red from years of henna. We could only dream of hair like Nargis's.

'Do you have a name for your doll?' she asked me. 'Barbie Doll,' I replied.

'Let's call her Rani,' she said. 'My father called me Rani when I was your age.'

So Barbie Doll became a princess. A rani.

When Nargis did laundry in the courtyard, she squatted near the water pump with a bucket and soap. Her hair poured like water over her shoulders, and her hips jiggled as she rinsed, wrung and hung the damp clothes on the line to air-dry. People would look at her as we scampered around the village for groceries and errands. Daddi often asked her to cover her head and bosom with a dupatta because there were men working around the house and it was a shameless thing to do, to try and distract them from work.

'Behaya aurat. She's a shameless woman,' Daddi said to Dadda one day. He nodded along, but I caught him looking at her. I caught him looking at her often.

The maids whispered the same foul things about Nargis. They wondered why both her husbands had left her. What must she have done, besides not producing children? Why did her family not accept her back? But even in the midst of all these whispers, I could only see Nargis's beauty, her hair, her. One night, I was having trouble falling asleep with my Barbie Doll, my rani. Daddi and I shared a bed in the primary bedroom while Dadda slept in a separate room. I watched the whirring fan in the dim glow of the night-light and listened to Daddi's snores. After a while, I climbed down the bed and went up the barsati to see Nargis. Surely she would play with me and my Barbie Doll. There was faint music coming from her radio—I knew she was awake.

Halfway up the stairs, I heard movement in her room. Movement, accompanied by muffled cries and whispers. I saw a large shadow on the wall. Someone was coming downstairs. I darted back to the bedroom. The door was ajar: I recognized the figure as it stepped downstairs and into the light.

Five months passed in the village. I missed the first two months at my school, and upon my parents' orders from across the world, my grandparents enrolled me in English, math and science tutoring classes in a nearby city.

Nargis became a shadow. She only emerged from the barsati at night to do her errands. I watched her silhouette in the kitchen, kneading dough and stirring pots. She began to drape her body in a big shawl. She kept away from me. She would greet me when I ran into her but did not linger as she had before. She spoke no more of dolls and ranis.

'Nargis is a bad influence,' Daddi began to say. 'Play with the other maids. Play with Abida, Parveen or Shaheen.' But

Abida, Parveen and Shaheen did not know how to apply henna designs on my palms like Nargis. They did not hum Bollywood tunes like Nargis. They did not care about playing hide-and-seek like Nargis. They did not have hair like Nargis.

I discovered Nargis's secret on a weekend Daddi and I were alone in the house. She was standing on a ladder, trying to remove cobwebs from the dining room ceiling. The servants were away attending a wedding, and Daddi had sent Dadda to Karachi several days before to tend to my brothers. His departure was discreet and unceremonious. One night he was having dinner with us, and the next, Daddi packed his bag and sent him off.

Suddenly, Daddi slipped from the ladder and hurt her back. She moaned in pain on the floor, and I struggled to lift her writhing body.

'Run upstairs and call Nargis!' she pleaded.

I frantically ran up the stairs and found Nargis sitting up on her bed, trimming the ends of her hair by candlelight. She did not have a shawl wrapped around her body, just a thin kameez and shalwar. She sat there before me, fully present, fully visible, and for the first time in several weeks, I saw her clearly. Her belly was large, straining, swollen up like a balloon. As I entered the room, she saw me and quickly jumped to her feet, hastily draping a dupatta around her torso. Confused, I asked her why her stomach looked like that. I asked her if she was unwell. She did not answer. She wanted to know why I was in her room.

'Daddi wants you downstairs,' I said. 'She hurt herself.'

'Let's go then.'

That weekend, Nargis ceased to be a shadow. She bustled around the house taking care of Daddi, who could do little to nothing in her condition. I tailed Nargis as she went about her chores, trying to get a peek at her protruding belly, though she tried to hide it whenever she saw me.

When Daddi caught a glimpse of Nargis's figure in the daylight, she called her names: a loose woman, a prostitute. Her anger and hostility were so fierce that she did not care if I was present or not. She could not contain herself. She wanted the ground to split open and swallow Nargis alive. She wanted her to drown in a well, to be buried in a desert. Away from her. Away from Dadda. Away from me. Away from the village. And away from memory.

'I'll send you away. I want you gone from this house!' Daddi yelled at her.

'Don't send me away, baji, don't send me away,' Nargis begged Daddi. 'I've no place to go. My family will kill me.' We were sitting in the courtyard on low bamboo stools.

I was snipping coriander on a steel tray. Nargis was slicing onions and tomatoes for lunch.

'I'm not a whore, baji,' said Nargis softly. 'Ask him. Ask him what happened.'

Daddi did not respond. She sat resolutely on her charpoy, an angry look clouding her face.

'Why don't you ask him?' Nargis repeated.

I did not know then whom Nargis was speaking about, but my grandmother did. She understood everything. As if she were not injured at all, she darted up from her seat and slapped Nargis hard across her face. The cutting board and the sliced vegetables fell to the ground.

I dropped my scissors and rose in fear. I had never seen my grandmother like that, so savage, so mad, so unrecognizably violent. A deep red spread across Nargis's cheek. She placed a hand on the bruise, bowed her head in shame and began to weep.

Daddi did not stop there—she grabbed my fallen scissors and reached for Nargis's braid.

'No, no!' Nargis wailed as she struggled to fight back. In the commotion, her hand accidentally hit Daddi on the forehead.

'Accha? So you want to hit me now?' Daddi exclaimed.

'Daddi, no!' I protested, shuddering. I wanted to move but found I couldn't. The courtyard, the bamboo stools, the charpoy, the vegetables: everything but Daddi disappeared at that moment. I watched her madness, afraid that if I moved, she would smack me across my face or shove me across the courtyard. I was afraid that she would hurt me too.

Eventually, Nargis stopped struggling and slumped down, defeated. Maybe my grandmother was stronger in every way, or maybe Nargis did not fight hard enough. Maybe she felt she deserved what was happening.

It took a while for the blades to work through her thick hair, though the struggle only made Daddi's cuts more ferocious. There was a tense stillness as she worked, broken only by the sharp, deafening sounds of snipping and tearing that filled the courtyard. And then, it was over. Nargis's braid fell to the ground like a dead snake. When she was done, my grandmother threw down the scissors victoriously and they hit the floor with a clank, right next to Nargis's hair. Her beautiful, dead hair.

Nargis sat still. Her hand moved slowly towards her neck. Her fingers felt the jagged, rough edges where the braid had been. Nargis looked at me. Her eyes said nothing. Her lips said nothing. And I said nothing in return. I don't know what she expected from a child, if she even expected anything at all, but I gave her nothing because I understood nothing. Why did Daddi do what she did? I wondered. Why did Nargis say what she had said?

I waited for Nargis to shriek. She had to shriek. Had to acknowledge, in some way, the horror of what had just happened. A part of me wanted her to rip Daddi apart, to curse Dadda loudly, but she didn't. She remained silent. Imperfect. Reduced to a shadow again. After a few seconds, Nargis wiped her tears, picked up her hair from the floor and tossed it in the trash.

The weekend ended. The help returned. Nargis vanished to the barsati once more.

⁂

One night, I woke up to the sound of someone crying. Like a stray cat wailing in the hallway. I hopped out of bed and followed the desperate sound. It was coming from upstairs. I went up to check and peeked into the barsati.

There, Nargis sat on the floor: her hair chopped, her legs wide apart, her face distorted in an expression of grief and pain. A strange woman sat on her knees by her side, shushing her, calming her, wiping sweat from her forehead with a small towel as she screamed. The woman saw me standing by the door and asked me to leave. I did not. I could not. My feet would not move. I was entranced by the scene before me, by Nargis's grunting, by the chaos. The woman asked me to leave again, her words sharp this time. I returned downstairs, bewildered.

As I lay in bed, waiting for nothing, I thought I heard another cry. A low cooing. A baby. I paused to listen, willing my heartbeat to quieten. But I could not hear a cry the second time, just Nargis, whimpering softly. I found it hard to fall back asleep, but when I finally did, I dreamt of a child playing with me in the sunny courtyard of our village home.

In the early hours of the morning before the servants arrived, I heard chattering outside the bedroom. I recognized the voices, Daddi and Nargis, and scrambled out of bed to peer through the slightly opened door. Nargis held a duffel bag in one hand and a piled-up blanket in the other. She swayed ever so gently as if trying to rock the quiet, unstirring bundle in her arms. As if she were trying to pacify herself. I never saw what was inside that blanket, but whatever it was, it never moved or made a sound. It remained still.

When Daddi saw me standing barefoot by the bedroom door, she told me to say goodbye to Nargis, who would be leaving us. I did not cling to Nargis as I said goodbye, as I might have before. Without her hair, she was a different thing. Frail, and small. I never asked why she left.

A tonga pulled up in front of the house, and Nargis sat down on the bench. As the horse trotted away, I watched Nargis, her eyes downcast. She was like an old photograph, a water stain, a dust of light under an almond tree.

⁂

Sakina and Shabana left after dinner. I warmed the bathroom with the electric heater and filled two plastic buckets of water for Daddi's bath. I removed her sweater and kameez and untied her silver hair. I rubbed red soap all over her body.

'Quratulain,' said my grandmother.

I paused. Water had brought her back to me, flooding the grey matter between the two hemispheres of forgotten time. She remembered everything about me in that hour. She asked me about my health. She asked me about the health of an old friend with whom I had lost touch. She asked me about my husband.

'I'm not married anymore, Daddi.'

'Accha, accha,' she said. 'That's a shame. Where are your children?'

'I don't have any.'

'Hmm.'

'I couldn't have any.'

'That's a pity. It's a long, empty life without a child.'

She then asked me where her own husband was, and I knew I had lost her once more. I rested my hands, which were gently scrubbing her back and arms. I collected myself, squeezed the bottle of Bio Amla shampoo and massaged it into her silver hair.

'You don't have to look for him anymore, Daddi,' I said. 'You don't have to mourn for him. He was not a good man.'

Daddi stayed very still as I continued bathing and talking to her.

'She had nothing. You were a woman. You were not good to her,' I said quietly. 'We were not good to her.'

I poured water on her back and washed the soap off. 'I could have done something. I could have said something, years ago. I was small, but I did nothing,' I said. 'And this is how I am living now—with nothing. And this is how you will live now, too.'

I do not know if my words reached her, but I told myself that they did. Her silence spoke volumes, her stillness revealed the truth.

'Accha, accha,' she said, finally.

She sat on a low stool, naked. I squatted near her, gently scrubbing her back and shoulders as she kept pouring warm water on herself. A cleansing ritual of a kind. An atonement, of a kind.

It Will Follow You Home

1

You describe Abigail's death to a Middle Eastern mental health counsellor. This is your fourth visit to the university's Centre for Psychological Services. She is your third therapist. You had never seen her wandering through the corridors before.

Then again, why should you have seen her?

You are someone who drops in for a biannual check-in after a depressive episode, tells your story to a new counsellor, and never returns the centre's calls for the next appointment. The only difference between then and now is that before, you were an MFA candidate struggling with a poetry thesis, and now, you are a lecturer of composition and rhetoric, struggling with a poetry collection.

'They're too white. The therapists in this town are too white for me,' you tell everyone. Your office mate. Your thesis director. Omar. Jeffery.

You also told this to Abigail. You were both sitting on her porch. She was helping you with your teaching portfolio. She brought a cigarette to her lips and reflected. You allowed the smoke from her cigarette to consume you and your view of the Lutheran church. She emitted a low chuckle.

You were both haunted.

Two months later, in November, you are to attend her memorial in the same oddly shaped red-brick church.

You do not like the sofa in the Middle Eastern counsellor's office. It makes a lot of noise when you move. And you move a lot. You try to sit still so she does not track your level of discomfort, your anxiety, by how many times you shift on the couch.

Behind her, evening expands rapidly in the purple-feathered sky. Fall in Morgantown, West Virginia, is a passionate time. You see the bright reds and burnt oranges from the window. The daylight escapes sooner. It gets dark earlier. And you hate that.

It terrifies you.

You look at the therapist's cluttered desk. A small crystal swan figurine on the corner of the table catches your eye. One of its wings is missing.

The therapist's brown fingers move swiftly on the notepad as you continue talking, and she continues to listen. You talk about your mother. About your brother in Cleveland. About your incomplete poetry collection. About your break-up with a good man weeks ago. About your habit of lingering in bad relationships.

You look down at your brown hands. They are dry.

You look over at the therapist's desk and shelves for moisturizer. Morgantown has made your skin dry. You always carry a small bottle of lotion, a travel-size Aveeno. You wake up in the middle of the night to apply and reapply it on your feet and hands. It is a ritual reserved only for America.

When you were twelve, your grandmother made a paste of gram flour, lemon juice and turmeric in a bowl. She spread it all over your face, your neck, your hands. The remedy, she promised, would give you fair and rosy skin, like your mother and sister. It never worked.

The therapist says she will call you back. You leave her office.

There is reassurance in her voice.

In the car you tell your friend Jeffery that you feel the same gravitational pull towards the Middle Eastern therapist that your Arab and Indian students feel towards you as a teacher. You call this pull 'the connection of brown skin'.

'The brown students seek me out.'

Jeffery does not think you should speak of skin colour so much. You tell him you never did before coming here.

His new therapist is a white man who teaches him activities to help him love himself. Your therapist gave you no such activity.

Jeffery tells you that, like other things in life, therapy is also a journey.

It is a wild flight.

2

Lahore is a delicious city. A mottled mess of vanishing history and new regimes. Lahore becomes ominous when you are in Morgantown. Lahore becomes a quiet mirage, an odd spectacle hung in time that only moves how you want it to move. It only moves when you want it to move. It does not speak to you or wail for you, yet you write only about Lahore. You preserve it in your poetry. You suppress it in a verse. You capture it in the refrain of a poem: its beating heart, its howls and cries, its chuckle. Yes, Lahore chuckles. The colonial drawing room in your mother's house. The pale light that slithered through the bedroom curtains. The moth your father captured in his palm when you were a child. And then he kissed the brown wings to show you that the moth was a friend. The goodness of the gardener who gave you jasmine flowers every evening. The ceramic bowl with painted tulips where you placed the flowers. The horrid monsoon rains that killed the houseboy. How long can a stanza sustain the scuffling of a city?

It's called being in love, your brother replies when you send him a text. *You do not like everything about the lover, yet you never really leave them. You keep returning one way or the other.*

Your brother wants you to stay in America. Find work in New York. Boston. DC. Virginia. Big places. Get out of Morgantown. Stay away from Lahore.

You are unable to do either.

Nothing ever happens in these places, he texts. You will never meet anyone.

He knows you linger in bad relationships.

America does not need foreign teachers who teach English composition, you text him. *Teachers who come with the burden of visas and visa fees.*

He does not reply. Doctors sleep early.

Whenever your mother calls you from Lahore, she speaks to you of returning. She tells you that you have left a clamouring city for a frozen town. You left a house with servants for a small apartment with dead succulents. Days go by. No one visits you. You pass Thanksgiving break and the summer holidays by yourself.

You tell your mother the story of Joyce Carol Vincent. A woman who died in her London apartment while watching television and packing gifts during the Christmas season. The housing officials discovered her body after two years. She was a skeleton. The television was still flickering. No one noticed her vanish.

Your mother does not like such stories. Omar said the same thing when you told him about Joyce. He took the spare apartment key from you. He said he would find your body the next day.

You won't be a skeleton.

And it won't be after two years.

You tell your mother that you are not mad at Lahore. If Lahore disappoints, Morgantown disappoints too. If Lahore makes your hair frizzy, Morgantown sucks the life out of your skin. You can't explain things you do not understand yourself. 'What are you running away from?' your mother asks you over the phone. Her voice is solemn.

She never asks your brother that.

You tell her that you were in Lahore for a long time. And when you left, you did not abandon it. You did not stop loving it. You left because of the noise. There was always too much noise in Lahore.

You tell her you will think about returning after Abigail's memorial.

3

You had never heard of melatonin before you moved to Morgantown. You read about the drug on a friend's Facebook status. You praised the metaphor in a friend's poem. Then, you saw it in CVS. Three milligrams. Five milligrams. Ten milligrams. *Fall asleep faster. Stay asleep longer.* Pills. Gummies. Bottles with moon and clouds, teddy bears and blankets, fruits and foliage.

You had heard of Lexotanil. Your mother took it to sleep. Your aunt took it after her husband died. Another aunt took it after her son drowned in Rawal Lake on his school trip. The women in your family took Lexotanil to escape.

Years ago, your brother gave you something called Clonazepam. It calmed you down. A boy had broken your heart. You had not stopped crying for months.

When you first moved to Morgantown three years ago, you met Omar and the group. You befriended the two Pakistani boys and three Indian girls because you wanted to speak to someone in Urdu. Your tongue craved it. Especially after a long day of teaching composition and rhetoric and sitting in a graduate poetry workshop. It was like having dessert after a three-course meal you did not relish but paid a lot to eat.

In the summer of 2016, you stayed up until 5 a.m. every day with the boys and watched Bollywood films and listened to Coke Studio songs.

Omar had lived in Karachi all his life. You were older than him. You were older than all of them. You lingered and stayed until 5 a.m. because you hated going back to your apartment. You had trouble sleeping in a new place. You had trouble waking up to stillness.

When the group was ready to retire, you would call an Uber. Omar would stand on the balcony of his apartment and watch you get into the car.

As the car drove by the mosque, the gas station, the recreation center, the laundromat, you would look up at the towering apartments. You pictured the tenants sleeping serenely under their blankets without melatonin.

4

You tell Jeffery in the English Department about how you are older than all your brown friends and how they keep joking about it. You are both making copies of midterm rubrics for your students.

He reminds you that you are still in your mid-twenties. You tell him old age comes faster for Pakistani women.

5

In the beginning of your relationship, Omar made you watch *Interstellar* with him. He loved the emergency docking scene where Matthew McConaughey manoeuvres the spinning spacecraft to match the rotation of the *Endurance*. McConaughey gets dizzy midway. Anne Hathaway passes out due to g-force. The Hans Zimmer score playing in the background gets louder, intensifying the stakes. You understand the symbolic meaning behind the scene because you studied literature, and because you are a poet. You conducted a little rhetorical analysis for Omar. You said the two spinning machines had meaning. The little spacecraft trying to match the momentum of the *Endurance* had meaning. The fainting of the astronauts had meaning too. He nodded and said he understood. You don't think he did.

6

In small towns, where there is a dearth of good coffee shops, there is also a dearth of good lovers. You get what you get. On Tinder. On Bumble. A game of beer pong at a frat party. In the mixers section at Ashebrooke Liquor Outlet. At a cricket screening potluck party. And then, you make the most of it. You pass the snow days. And the fall days. And the two days of summer.

7

You live on campus. You are a twenty-six-year-old lecturer who lives on campus. Abigail lived on campus too. You walk by her house every day. You do not see her smoking on her porch anymore.

You cannot avoid walking by her house, the same way you cannot avoid stopping by Omar's apartment whenever you go for a jog, which is every evening.

He lives five minutes away.

You cannot reason with this addiction anymore. You cannot explain why you do this, again and again. You cannot explain to your therapist why you keep meeting Omar when he was the one who ended the relationship. To Jeffery. To your brother. Maybe because there is no one else left for you in this town. So you lie and tell everyone you're not seeing him.

8

You call Jeffery one midnight to speak about white space.

In stories, it is the emptiness between lines and characters and passages, you tell him. A vacancy. Stillness.

If done right, the reader catches a break.

If overdone, things are misplaced and forgotten.

You tell him that when you leave a place, physically or metaphorically, there are plenty of white spaces.

Between you and the new characters, you and the people and the places that were left behind, between past and present. Maybe a white space is an hour to yourself. A bath you draw. A talk with a stranger that leads nowhere. Packing bags and moving to a new place. It is leaving things for a moment and returning to them.

Returning for them. Or maybe perhaps never returning at all and finding other things.

'Why is white space necessary?' you ask Jeffery over the call. 'It gives you a minute to breathe. It shows you your place by making you lose your place for a moment.'

There is silence on the other end. Then, Jeffery asks if you dreamt of Lahore again.

9

You have a habit of stealing things from your brother's apartment. He barely notices when things go missing.

Doctors are busy people. Doctors are rich people. His life has meaning.

You take all the left-behind quarters. You pick up the candles that are forgotten. You take the books he will never read. You take the medicines he brought back from Pakistan. Panadol for fever. Ponstan Forte for period pain. Skinoren gel for acne marks.

You always come to Cleveland with an empty bag. You pay thirty dollars at airports for an empty bag, but you return home to Morgantown with a suitcase full of things.

You use the quarters for laundry. And you light the candles when you are writing poetry at night.

10

You wonder if your friends in Lahore ever think of you. They never call.

There is a magic about small towns. It feels as though, somehow, you can possess them in the palm of your hand. The town's history. Its trees. Its people. People know when you go missing. Many heard about Abigail's fall.

Cities are unfaithful.

11

Jeffery tells you that his West Virginian twang comes out in conversations sometimes. You tell him Lahori people have a unique accent too. Omar often reminds you when you sound like a Lahori.

12

Your mother reminds you that you are on a visa. She reminds you that you are not free.

'Remember in December of 2016, when you were visiting Lahore and there was that Muslim ban and you were not sure if you will ever return to Morgantown to finish your MFA? Do you remember? Do you want to live in such a country?'

She asks you to return. Again, and again.

You were supposed to be your mother's third child. She had two miscarriages before, followed by a long period of waiting before, finally, you arrived. You have always given her so much pain.

When you failed your eighth-grade exams, she took time off from work to teach you. She lost her job. You were terrible in school. You were terrible in Quran class. You were terrible at sports.

You were only ever good at writing. In making up stories about why you were not good at anything.

13

You tell your therapist the full story of your break-up over the summer. The white essential oil diffuser on her windowsill releases a mist. Perhaps it smells of rain and eucalyptus. You want the fragrance to reach you. It never does.

You apply moisturizer on your dry hands and look at the crystal swan figurine while telling the therapist how much rage you have in your body. How you shriek in your apartment and wail and howl like a child in pain.

Omar, now just a friend, often grabs you by your shoulder and asks, 'Where do you get so much anger in that little body?'

Once he picked up a bottle of water and sprayed it on you as if trying to perform an exorcism.

You have always been angry. You were an angry child.

You are an angry adult. You are an angry lover.

You tell the therapist about your lonely summer in Morgantown. Your Pakistani and Indian friends graduated and left. Jeffery went to Beckley to meet his family. Omar called you from Karachi to break up over the phone.

The therapist says what Jeffery says, what your brother says, what Omar says: Face it and move on.

You ask her if you can take Omar to Abigail's memorial. It won't be a date.

'Has anything changed between you two since the break-up? Since he returned?'

You tell her that he has put on weight, and you have stopped writing poetry.

14

Writing is like building a house. You lay the foundation. You erect the building. You make the windows and the doors. And then you return for the plumbing and the electrical wires. The carpets and the kitchen counters. The revision.

You graduated six months ago. You submitted your MFA thesis in May. It is now mid-October. You have not fixed any leakages or rusty pipes since then.

15

Saba, a friend back home, married young because she wanted to be a good-looking bride. You scroll through her photos on Facebook. She had her second child and is visiting Paris soon. Her marriage was arranged. Your mother is also finding you a suitable arrangement.

Saba sent you a Facebook message after reading your sentimental post about Abigail's death. She asks ordinary random questions about Abigail. You give ordinary random answers back about Abigail. Then, Saba writes: *Any good news from your side?*

You look at her recent profile photo. Her belly is swollen. Her hair is short and cropped and bleached blonde. A toddler is holding her right hand.

Not yet, you write back. *What did you name your new baby?*

16

The Middle Eastern therapist asks why Abigail was important to you.

'She wasn't,' you reply. 'At least when she was alive. I barely knew her. I met her properly twice in her life.'

You tell her that Abigail became important after she died. The therapist nods.

'Does that make sense?'

Does that make sense? Does that make sense?

She nods again.

'It's a strange place to be in,' you continue. 'A strange liminal space. When you know them just enough that their death rattles you, impairs you in a way, but not so much that it drives you mad.'

'There's no rulebook for mourning,' replies the therapist. 'But she had it in her, you know. She had it in her. All the shadows. All the shadows I have inside of me.'

The therapist asks you to explain what you mean. You search for moisturizer in your purse.

Abigail taught and wrote just like you. Abigail existed in liminal spaces just like you. Abigail could not write, just like you. She carried the noise in her. It followed her places. You do not tell the therapist any of these things, but instead say, 'That swan over there. Why is its wing missing?'

The therapist makes a confused face and looks behind at her desk. 'Oh, when did that happen? I never noticed.'

17

Jeffery tells you often how sophisticated and beautiful you are.

You show him a picture of a white swan on Google Images. Gliding gracefully, smoothly on the surface. The struggle, the oddities, the madness, the melatonin, the Middle Eastern therapist, the drying hands, the falling hair, unfinished poems, the noise, Abigail, Omar, Lahore, the flapping webbed legs underneath the water.

No one sees that.

18

You buried dead birds all summer. You have seen various crime scenes by now. Eyes wide open. Flies paying homage.

Legs stiffened and up in the air. Blood splattered behind the little head. A wing missing. Both wings missing.

Death is chaotic. Death is unreal. Death is necessary.

19

News arrives from Lahore. It comes in the middle of class.

Your parents moved out of your childhood home.

You didn't pick up your calls. I think you're teaching, your father texts. *I'm sending you some photos of the old house as we are driving away.*

20

News from Morgantown.

You send another desperate email to your supervisor, writing that you want a work visa for next year. She does not promise anything. The department does not sponsor international faculty for long periods.

21

You have never made a good cup of chai in Morgantown. Omar says that this is because you never measure anything. You never measure the cups of water, the spoonfuls of tea leaves or sugar. Making chai is an art.

Many things have changed about Omar since he returned from Karachi. He now serves you what he calls doodh pati, milk tea, the ugly stepsister of chai. He boils tea leaves in milk instead of water.

You detest it, just like you now detest him.

You tell him his doodh pati is making your hair fall out. You tell him his doodh pati is causing acne breakouts on your forehead. You tell him his doodh pati gave you depression and that is why you are seeing a therapist and that is why you have not written anything in three months.

Omar does not reply. He just listens. You have hurt him like this so many times. He never says anything in return. He finds other ways to hurt you.

22

The body is rarely silent. Even in death, there is tumult. Even after the body becomes unlovely and free, there is suppressed murmuring of the soul. Under the dirt. Under the dust. Under all that rubble. There is no such thing as the end, your mother tells you that over the phone.

Life does not end after you die. Even in dead things, there is a shard of life tucked away somewhere.

It is 9 a.m. in Morgantown and your mother is speaking about heaven, hell and the transience of life. On speakerphone, she is telling you about the ultimate test of man during the uproarious Judgement Day. When God calls you before Him and asks you if you have been good in the world. Your mother, father, Quran teacher, aunts and uncles have told you many times what 'good' means.

You put on a sweater and wrap a shawl around your neck.

You are preparing to head out.

'I am praying that you come out of this. I am praying for your sadness,' she says. A sadness, she affirms, which will pass once you move back to Lahore.

You tell her that it won't pass. It will follow you home. It stays. It stays. It stays.

And it has no name.

She tells you that whatever it is, you got it from your father's side of the family.

'Think big,' she says. 'Think of the afterlife. Don't do anything stupid in this life.'

You wish you had not told her how Abigail died. 'Mama, I have to go to work. I have to go teach.'

You think of your mother as you drive to the Caperton Trail in the evening. You stand by the edge and look down at the Monongahela River. You heard Abigail had wanted to drown in those dark waters.

23

You ask Omar for the fifth time if it is over. He tells you for the last time that it is. You ask him what happened in Karachi with his family. He does not reply. You take a long puff from your cigarette and kill it near his feet. You bought him those shoes. You tell him how much you hate his mother.

24

'Are you in a crisis? Are you in danger?' the therapist asks you.

You tell her no, but that you do understand why some writers kill themselves.

25

An acquaintance sends out a formal email about Abigail's memorial. It is one week away. Her photograph is pasted in the email. You are sitting in the library. You post the reminder in your Google calendar. You set an alarm on your phone. You send a text to Omar reminding him when and where the memorial is, and you tell him that you do not want him to come.

You cry in the library bathroom. A girl washes her hands and exits. She does not pacify you. This is not the restroom of a bar.

You return to your chair. There is a leak in the ceiling of the reading room. You wonder if Abigail's ghost has left the building. You wonder if her ghost ever left Morgantown.

26

The sky grumbles as you take the I-79 north to Cleveland. It is 3 a.m. It is December and everything you ever owned is either at Goodwill or in the car.

You left no messages for Omar or your therapist. You did not pass by Abigail's house or the red-brick church. You did not write a follow-up email to your supervisor or send a sentimental voicemail to Jeffery. You could not bring yourself to attend Abigail's memorial. You left without noise.

As you drive out of the town in the dark, the check engine light comes on. You pull the car to the side of the lonely highway. Morgantown is not too far behind. Maybe it wants you to stay.

You switch off the engine and let the car rest for a minute. There is rustling in the tree line on the side. You wait for a deer or a raccoon to emerge, but instead, a different creature comes out.

It is a swan.

A spectacular white swan in the dead dark night.

You roll down your window to hear the scuffling, the rustling, the yapping. But there is a dreadful silence, a dreadful space.

For a few moments, you don't breathe, you don't blink, you don't exist. You sit quietly in the car and let the swan cross, let it take its time.

Stray Things Do Not Carry A Soul

Daddy worked many jobs, but Daddy liked his night job best. He liked shooting stray dogs in the streets.

Every morning he swept the roads, painted dull pavements, and unclogged jammed gutters in Victoria Colony, and every evening he slung the shotgun over his shoulder, left the servant quarters, and went into the dimming alleys looking for dogs. He told me it was okay to hunt them down because they were feral. Borderline mad. They were no one's anything. They had no mothers. No one wailed for them after they were gone. They were stray, and stray things did not carry a soul.

When November arrived, I dropped out of school and began accompanying my father to work. My mother was furious. She had been dreaming of a better future for me. One where I had a proper job. She did not want me raking leaves in a rich man's red-brick bungalow or playing cricket in the garden with his son, who only spoke in English—she envisioned better lives, lives that required schooling. Perhaps I could have been a well-dressed clerk at a government office, or an IT specialist at an English medium school like my mother's younger brother, Aslam. He had taken a computer training course after his BA exams.

'I don't shop at the landa bazaar now,' Aslam had said on his last visit to our servant quarter. We were sitting on charpoys in the small open courtyard drinking chai. I noticed he was wearing a green and white plaid dress shirt.

Aslam Mamu was a big man now. 'I shop at the mall. Never the flea market again.'

Amma liked her brother's new extravagance. She watched him prosper—with fascination. It was something she had never been granted growing up—a chance to leap, make mistakes, fix them and leap again. A chance to find herself and find out what she was good at besides squatting and sweating profusely before a gas stove, making parathas and aloo methi or chana and white rice. Amma had many resentments.

Mother was married off at fifteen to her distant cousin, my father, who lived in the same village in Hafizabad. Neither had attended school. Mother was a liability, and she would say that liabilities in her family were not sent to schools or colleges, but bundled up and wedded off to cousins who worked or old widowers who needed young brides to make them dinner and tend to their ailing bodies.

Daddy told me he left school when he was seven because he didn't like his strict math teacher who hit students' palms with a wooden ruler when they got the multiplication tables wrong. Daddy dashed back home one day, leaving behind his satchel and lunchbox on the school bench. From then on, it was lifting wheat sacks at a warehouse with his older brothers.

Mother had shoved Daddy out of the village to Lahore for a better life after they married. She had my sister, Rashda, at sixteen, lost five children after that (one died during birth, two strangled themselves in the womb, and two frail twins survived only a year), and then had me, a boy. A miracle child. Mother would say she had me after visiting various shrines, wearing multiple amulets, and falling at the feet of many colourful saints.

'Mera beta,' Amma would sing. 'My beautiful little son. It was the big pir's prayer that blessed me with you, Haider Ali. Don't become a useless and soulless man like your father. Learn from your Aslam Mamu.'

Daddy never cared for my uncle's new lifestyle, and didn't like when he visited. Daddy did not like his leather belts and shoes. He didn't like his ironed dress shirts, the rented two-room house, or his new wife, who always wore a bright pink lipstick.

Once, Daddy and I watched Aslam Mamu speed away on his Honda CD70 motorbike after he had finished telling us about his shopping mall trips. Daddy had furrowed his eyebrows and spat his paan in the open alley sewer outside the quarter. The servant quarters were lined with tin doors, red spit stains and cigarette butts.

'Sister-fucker,' Daddy muttered in Punjabi.

If my uncle was a successful man, my father was a proud one.

⌘

I did not know who I wanted to be at the age of ten.

I did not know if I wanted to be like Aslam Mamu, whizzing and zooming through Lahore on my gleaming Honda, or to be like Daddy, with a pack of Morven cigarettes, ambling through colonial bungalows with jasmine vines and Rangoon creepers on walls, holding a broom for sweeping or a thick bamboo stick for blocked drains and gutters.

What I did know was that I wanted a life somewhat similar to that of the little boy in Bungalow 17.

He was seven.

He had a blue bicycle which he rode around the circular driveway of the colonial house, went to school in a huge black car with a green government number plate, and called his father 'Daddy.' After I heard him sing 'Daddy, Daddy, Daddy' in the corridors of the bungalow and the driveway, I began to call my father that too.

My father had taken me to Bungalow 17 several times. He was a part-time worker there. He washed the driveway, helped the gardener trim the hedges, and had lunch in the kitchen with the driver, Samandar Khan.

The mistress needed extra help around the house and was looking for an errand boy, so my father took me there one day and offered my services. The mistress stood on the porch wrapped up in a black shawl with red embroidered flowers and looked down at me. She asked why I wasn't at school.

'How can a poor man like myself pay for two kids' school?' my father began. 'And he says he doesn't want to go to school either.'

'The driver said you have an older daughter too,' she said. 'Does she go to school?'

'Yes, madam. She's sixteen. She's sitting for her matriculation exams in May.'

'I can pay for the boy's expenses if he goes to school,' the mistress offered, looking down at me. I could tell from her face that she was impressed by my sister and a little disappointed in me.

Jealousy stirred in me. I felt about Rashda what my father felt about my uncle.

'Speak, boy,' Daddy nudged me jokingly. 'Would you go to school if Madam pays?'

'I'd go to school if I could go in a big car like that'—I pointed at the black Land Cruiser Samandar Khan was cleaning.

Daddy smacked my head. The mistress chuckled and went into the bungalow through the screen door.

She had said I was hired.

Neither my mother nor my sister was too pleased with my new job at a big railway officer's bungalow. They were not enthralled by the five-bedroom house, the sprawling lush garden and backyard with pink bougainvillea and purple dahlias, or my salary of two thousand rupees that could buy me a sturdy cricket bat but never the blue bicycle Muhammad Daniyal had. I dreamed of riding it.

Daddy told them I was on a fast track to becoming a mard—a man. And if I continued working hard, I could soon buy a bicycle and a cell phone.

'Not a mard,' Rashda said with a mouthful of red lentils and white rice. 'A naukur.'

Naukur.

A servant.

Amma cast Daddy a stern, unkind look. There was repugnance in her eyes. It was as if she was accusing him of her only son's failure. She looked at my father as if he was the bad seed in our family. The rotten apple. The corrupt, bad fish that could spoil the whole pond. She had said many times that if Daddy did not start bringing his entire salary home instead of spending it on other dangerous things, she would end up cleaning people's houses and washing their clothes.

'This is your miracle child, Amma,' Rashda derided. 'Washing an officer's car and brooming dirty verandas. All that money you wasted for the three classes at school he barely passed.'

Amma lifted the steel lid from the pressure cooker to pour lentils on her plate. Steam unfurled from the cooker and she disappeared behind the white fog. I was glad I could not see her disdain.

Rashda meant every cruel, callous word she uttered.

We were both put in the same school in the crowded, humming Dharampura neighbourhood near Victoria Colony. The lowly English medium school building with chipping white paint and growing grey-green mould was nestled between a meat market and a shop selling brassieres and whitening creams.

Rashda stayed in school and moved to high school. I gave up and fled. She said I couldn't make it because I was too stupid, like all the illiterate men in our family. And there were many. Amma would count them on her fingers as examples to me.

Rashda's mockery made my body rattle with anger, but I knew I had another way of getting back.

'Your husband is also a fifth fail,' I reminded her. 'He'll be a servant too, and you'll also make rotis in his kitchen like Amma.'

Rashda's smile drooped. She stopped eating and turned her troubled face away from me. I had aimed straight for the jugular.

She had been betrothed to our cousin, Rehan, when she was only six—a common tradition in our family. A solemn pledge of child betrothal between solemn relatives at solemn hours, before a child could even comprehend her existence.

I suspected my sister was interested in another boy, who went to evening classes with her. I had caught a handwritten letter in one of her science books. I could not understand what it said, but there was a heart with an arrow drawn at the centre of the writing. I had also seen her getting dropped off on a stranger's motorbike when Daddy was not around.

'It's my friend's brother,' she clarified once. 'I didn't have money for a rickshaw. Don't get stupid ideas.'

Daddy's face turned red. 'Get up.' He signalled for me to rise from the kitchen floor where I sat with my plate of rice. 'Come with me.'

He steered me away from the disappointed women, past the courtyard and into the darkening alley outside. All the doors of the other servant quarters were shut. A Bollywood song played loudly on someone's television set. A group of young boys stood at the mouth of the alley smoking cigarettes and watching a video of a gyrating woman on a mobile phone.

Daddy and I walked around the colony in silence. I heard the repressed squeaking and twittering of birds and bats in old trees. I watched the suspended shotgun dance on Daddy's right shoulder as he fished out the pack of Morvens and matchbox from his pocket.

Other municipal marksmen did their work of shooting stray dogs in the afternoons or evenings, hours when the daylight had not yet slipped. And they did it when there was a complaint of a growing stray population in the streets or when a feral, mad dog was spotted, frightening bungalow women taking evening strolls.

Daddy liked the darkness, and ignored the time and order for his shootings.

I noticed he liked to spend as little time as possible at home, probably because when he was outside, he could do whatever he liked. Be whatever he liked. The sweeper. The huntsman. My mentor. A friend.

At home, Amma ruled.

Outside, Daddy had friends, and those friends always had gifts wrapped in small plastic pouches for him. I don't know what they contained but the gesture made Daddy smile and firmly shake their hands. Daddy liked playing cards and betting crumpled hundred-rupee notes in the quiet park near the mosque.

Daddy pulled the long shotgun off his shoulder and handed it to me. I held it, afraid, gingerly, as if the gun were a sleeping baby. It was very heavy. He monitored my reluctance and grinned, displaying his deep red gums and decaying front teeth.

'It won't go off,' he assured me. 'And it shouldn't go off because you don't have this.'

He pulled out a plastic card from his front kameez pocket and proudly tapped at his signature on the firearms license near his black-and-white photo.

I could tell he was proud that he had a printed signature on the license instead of a thumbprint. He was not an angutha-chhaap—a jaahil, an unlettered man who was asked to sign important documents with a thumb impression instead of a signature.

Daddy came closer to me and said that he was also an important man like Aslam Mamu, no matter what Daddy's wife said. Would the government hand an unimportant man a shotgun and assign him the task of saving lives from mad, feral things?

'Bilkul nahi,' he shook his head, answering his own question. 'Your mother doesn't know anything. She just has a sharp tongue. A good woman doesn't talk too much.'

He often said things like that when we were alone. He would say the same thing about Rashda, that she had also begun talking too much.

I teetered after him with the gun. Daddy raised his hand, asking me to be still and stay back.

It was not time to shoot the dogs yet.

Once, I had asked one of Daddy's friends why they had to shoot the dogs in the city instead of just scaring them away.

'Do you know what happened to Chacha Rashid's youngest daughter?' Nisar had replied.

Nisar was a butcher in the market near my old school. He sold sickly white chickens during summer months, and displayed thawed rohu fish in winter.

I was sitting with Nisar, Daddy and an old man in the park, watching them gamble and play cards.

'Three dogs attacked the poor child,' Nisar continued. 'They couldn't find the rabies injection anywhere. There was foam coming from her mouth when she died the same night.'

'Last summer, another dog bit a sleeping woman's arm,' the old man spoke up. 'Her arm was dangling from the charpoy. These feral dogs are not afraid of humans like they were before. They have developed a taste for human flesh.'

'Do they also go to heaven or hell?' I asked. 'These stray dogs?'

'No one waits for them in heaven or hell,' said Daddy. 'No one wants them in the afterlife either.'

The three men reassured me that it was necessary to hunt and shoot. I had asked only because I'd grown quite fond of a black-and-white dog that lived in the scaffoldings of a construction site near Bungalow 17. A few times I'd tossed him roti and bone, leftovers from my lunch in the bungalow kitchen.

There was a black fur spot on the dog's white back that was shaped like a heart. Like the one in Rashda's letter.

Now, Daddy left me standing under a dim white streetlight with the shotgun. He disappeared behind a kikar tree. I could see that there were two other unfamiliar men waiting for him there.

I had seen Daddy do that many times, vanish behind a tree with his friends. In the early mornings, especially before he headed to work, and late evenings, before he began his culling spree. He would vanish behind a tree and resurface after a few long minutes without a word. I never asked him when he would return.

From the corner, I caught glimpses of the affair. There was a man tying a strap around Daddy's bare arm. The other cracked a loud joke in Punjabi as he held a syringe. I saw Daddy's arms get heavy. He leaned back against the tree. The rest of the scene was submerged in silence and shadows.

Dry leaves crunched under the men's feet. A dog barked in the distance.

After some time, the men dawdled away, leaving me with Daddy, who took the shotgun from my arms. He stood still for a few minutes, playing with the loose bullets in his pocket. They made low-pitched clinks as he fidgeted.

'Do you hear them?' His words slurred a little. He was looking into the distance, listening intently to something.

More nameless, unwanted dogs barked and howled around the colony.

'Talking, barking, talking, barking. Do you hear them, Haider Ali?'

I did.

'Yapping away like those women at home.'

Daddy was angry. He loaded the chamber with four bullets, cupped the barrel of the gun, and pulled it towards himself. Something clicked. He meandered in the direction of the sounds.

I followed and watched Daddy aim at a pack of dogs rummaging through a garbage dump. They did not seem mad or dangerous. He signalled to me to remain silent and cover my ears. He shot two bullets.

There were sounds of whining and scurrying. A bullet took down a brown dog. Daddy aimed and shot at it again. The lifeless body jolted and remained as it was, lifeless. Quiet. But there was blood splatter the second time. The road stained red.

'It's dead,' I said loudly, my hands still covering my ears. 'Why did you shoot it again?'

'We should be sure. Sometimes they don't die that easily.' I looked at the dead dog for some time. I could feel Daddy's eyes on me. I knew that if I cried, he would call me na-mard. He would tell me that I was not man enough. That I was a eunuch, a little girl.

My body tingled. I thought I saw the dead dog quiver. Daddy said it did not and then we moved on, looking for more dogs.

There was another difference between other colony marksmen and my father. They had become part-time shooters to feed their families in the servant quarters. Fifty rupees per dead dog, Nisar had told me. But Daddy, Daddy enjoyed the morbid task. He enjoyed loading the shotgun and asking me to cover my ears. He enjoyed aiming and watching the dogs tremble, fall, not dead, nearly dead, finally dead. He enjoyed the nighttime, the gunshots, the shuddering, the gargling, the holding on to life by a thread, and then the slow vanishing of life. It was like a melody to his ears or a game. A game he always won.

There was a submission in Daddy whenever we returned home together. It was as if he knew what he was. He could not cheat or bluff as he did with his friends or with the stray dogs when he beckoned them closer, hiding the shotgun behind his back.

Daddy told Nisar and the old man that once he was asked to join the Dolphin Force, the esteemed police force that patrolled Lahore at night curbing crime, but he chose not to join because it was too much work. I knew that was a lie. Outside the house, under the towering kikar, taali and lemon trees of Victoria Colony, with the sly bats, sleepless strays and effervescing shadows, Daddy unspooled. He was immortal.

⁂

The boy in Bungalow 17 was very special. Samandar Khan, the driver, told me one day that Muhammad Daniyal was a miracle child like me.

I was a regular at the bungalow now. I cleaned cars, corridors, and the white kitchen counters upon the maid's commands. It was only after I cleaned that she permitted me to eat lunch in the kitchen. Otherwise, it was the driveway or the wet garden.

I was sitting on my haunches in the driveway, cleaning the muddy tires and bumper of the Land Cruiser with a water hose, when Khan told me that the doctor made the bungalow boy in a glass dish in a hospital.

I asked how that was even possible and how he knew it was true. He said he drove Madam and Sir around Lahore, to different clinics, and understood some English words when they conversed.

'Everything's possible in today's world, son,' Samandar Khan said. 'Babies can be made inside dishes. I saw a YouTube video on my mobile where an Indian doctor was saying how a baby's gender can be chosen. Men can get their no-nos cut and become girls.'

I asked why my Amma had to lose so many children and gain so much weight to have me if doctors could have done something.

'But for money. Everything can be bought from paisa.' Samandar Khan lifted the wiper blades and began cleaning the windshield of the Land Cruiser. 'And we're poor people. We get what we get. Boy. Girl. Stillborn. Nothing. This disease. That disease.'

At that moment, the screen door on the porch flew open and the bungalow boy, Daniyal, hopped out with a cricket bat. It was time for us to play in the garden.

'Three hundred thousand rupees. That kid was made in three lakhs,' Samandar Khan jokingly winked. 'We can buy fifty of you in that sum, Haider Ali.'

Daniyal might have been a special child but, like me, he was also lonely. Since I'd left school, I rarely had anyone to play with on the streets. In the mornings, most of the children from the quarters left for school or their jobs, and in the afternoons and evenings, when they played marbles, cricket, or catch, I was either at the bungalow or out sweeping fallen leaves and juice boxes with Daddy.

Daniyal and I played for hours in the garden. Cricket, badminton and video games on the big television set in his room. We peered at his colourful books with pictures of insects and fruits. He had a big bedroom full of toy cars, racetracks, stuffed animals and every good thing I had ever seen.

'What insects can we catch in the garden in November?' he asked, flipping through the book, running his index finger over the bright pages and big bold English words.

I placed my hand next to his on the picture of a winged insect. I noticed how dark my hand was compared to his.

'D ... R ... A ... DRA ... G ... O ... GON ...' he mumbled the letters aloud as he tried to pronounce the insect's name. 'Dragonfly!'

I told him I had seen many in the unkempt bushes near the servant quarters.

'Fireflies, butterflies, dragonflies,' he said. 'They're all in the summer. What can we catch at this time?'

I pretended to think along with him as we flipped the glossy pages.

His daddy went to work in a new Toyota with an armed guard, and mine dove deep into gutters and shot dogs. His daddy taught him about fireflies and airplanes. Mine had begun asking me to scoop up the carcasses and put them in a cleanup truck.

Daniyal taught me how to write my name in English and how to count to twenty when we played hide-and-seek. I told him about my secret stray dog with a heart on its back, and that Daniyal was a lucky boy because he did not have a sister. I hated mine.

'Look at this'—Daniyal showed me something in his book. It was a picture of a forest at night, lit up with tiny fireflies. They were like little balls of fire floating in the trees and plants. It reminded me of when we had an open-fire stove in our quarters and Amma poked at the burning wood with tongs, sending sparks flying in the air, winged embers, like the fireflies in the book.

'When my grandmother died last year,' Daniyal said, 'my daddy said her soul will leave her body and reach heaven.'

I wondered what that would look like, a soul leaving a body. I wanted to picture it. Could I see the soul escaping up in the air when someone died?

'Maybe this is also what happens when your father shoots a dog,' said Daniyal, lying on the carpet, placing his hand under his chin and flipping through the insect book. 'The soul leaves the body like fireflies. Goes up and up and up like bright fireflies into the heavens.'

⁂

One Sunday, Aslam Mamu and his wife, Neelam, with the pink lipstick, took our family to Bagh-e-Jinnah Gardens for a picnic.

Mother and Rashda sat in the Honda carrying the picnic bundle, while Daddy, Neelam and I followed the laughing trio in a rickshaw which my uncle paid for.

Daddy sulked and put on a clean grey shalwar kameez for the occasion. He had disappeared behind the tree earlier for his mysterious ritual.

I could tell, all morning, as we waited in the courtyard and watched Amma and Rashda prepare food, that Daddy was not looking forward to my uncle's picnic.

We sat on a dastarkhwan on the grass. Aslam Mamu showed off his new camera mobile. It had a huge screen and took clear pictures. Rashda posed for a few photos and asked my uncle if she could print them because she had to show them to a friend.

Aslam Mamu told me that if I returned to school, I could buy a similar phone. Maybe even an expensive one.

'What's the issue?' Aslam Mamu asked as we all sat down on the tablecloth to eat. There was kindness in his eyes. 'Why did you leave school, Haider Ali?'

'I ... I ...' I stammered, not knowing if I wanted to tell him the truth: that I found the homework, the cramming of alphabets, words, the hours inside a classroom, and the blue uniform too dreary.

'Because he wasn't able to understand anything the teacher said,' Rashda chimed in.

'That's not true,' Daddy interjected. 'He could've if he stayed. He's intelligent. It was his decision.'

Aslam Mamu looked at my sister, then Daddy, and then back at me. 'Is it true? Do you find your studies hard?'

'No,' I lied. 'I don't. I understood everything in class.'

'I can teach you if you want,' Rashda offered.

I looked at her doubtfully, waiting for her to erupt in a burst of scornful, pitiful laughter. But her expression remained sincere.

'I know everything.'

'Tell us the multiplication table of two,' she challenged me. Daddy did not interfere the second time; instead, he looked at me, as Amma did, as Neelam did, as Rashda and Aslam Mamu did.

'Two times two is ...' I paused and looked at Daddy. I knew he wanted me to get it right for him, for us. 'Eight?'

Rashda and Uncle shook their heads. Rashda laughed. 'I can count to twenty in English.'

'A school is not everything,' Daddy finally said. 'I found him a job. He'll be standing up on his feet in no time.'

'Like you are? With your good job?' Amma said.

Daddy stopped eating after that. He gestured to me to rise and we left the picnic spot so he could smoke a cigarette by a tree. 'Does he still do nasha?' I overheard my uncle ask my mother.

'He'll never leave the drugs, and if he can't find money for it, he'll sell his family. There's rarely any money in the house now,' Amma said. 'There are complaints about him. Aslam, can you give me a thousand rupees for this week? I have to start asking our family for a loan.'

Neelam made a face when Aslam Mamu took out a stylish blue wallet to help Amma out.

'I don't want Haider to quit school,' I heard Rashda say. 'I don't want Haider to become like him.'

⁂

After finishing the curry, parathas and roasted corn and peanuts—Neelam's mouth smudged with pink lipstick (which Aslam Mamu tenderly wiped away with a tissue)—we left Bagh-e-Jinnah and made our way to a nearby market. There, after a brief stop, we crossed a busy road to where Aslam Mamu had parked his motorbike.

There was a rush of roaring traffic. Cars, rickshaws, motorbikes and street vendors choked the narrow neighbourhood road.

Rashda froze in the middle of the moving traffic and placed her hands over her ears, as I did when Daddy shot dogs. Ever since we were children, she had always carried a fear of busy roads. The blaring horns, the screeching sea of cars and the crashing rickshaws seemed to paralyze her.

A motorbike swerved, almost hitting her. The driver yelled out, calling her mad and blind.

'That's a woman,' Daddy snickered from the pavement. We stood and watched Aslam Mamu raise his hand and motion a clattering rickshaw to come to a halt so he could rescue my petrified sister.

'All they can do is say vile things, but by the end of the day only a man can save them,' Daddy said. 'That's the reality of a woman. All words. Nothing more.'

⌘

By January, I had fully immersed myself in my job at the bungalow. I had also grown closer to Muhammad Daniyal.

We began sneaking out during afternoons once his mother had stopped bustling in and out of rooms and had withdrawn to her bedroom for a nap.

We met the black-and-white dog in the scaffoldings. He was a friend now. I had been saving him from my father for months by distracting or rerouting him during hunting nights.

'He doesn't bite,' Daniyal often said. 'No, he doesn't.'

'And he is so soft.'

'So soft.'

'There really is a heart on its back.'

'There is.'

⌘

With the frosty air and the blinding winter fog, a new feeling festered within me. A seed was sown. I began to loathe the women in my house. Daddy spoke about Amma and Rashda with a relentless obsession. He said that he had been a good, pious teenager before he met Amma, who performed black magic on him so she could command the house. It was because of black magic that he was never in his senses and was now spending most of his hours sleeping in the park under trees. He should have married his cousin Nazia, his paternal uncle's pretty daughter.

'All women are churails,' he told me now and then. 'And these churails should be thrown in the canal.'

'Even the madam in the bungalow? She is a witch too?'

'Even her.'

'What about my old math teacher Farzana?'

'Her too. All of them.'

I could agree about Rashda, Amma and even Miss Farzana, who always twisted my ear in class and asked if I was paying attention, but my heart was not convinced that Daniyal's mother was a witch. She was too beautiful to be a churail. With her rosy cheeks that resembled the delicate petals of a gulab, her painted nails and her beautiful shawls, how could she be one? How could she be one when she asked me to scrub my feet before entering the living room because she did not like the carpets dirty?

Over the following wintry weeks, Daddy became nocturnal. He disappeared behind the tree a lot. There were days his breath was strangely pungent. I couldn't tell what he had eaten. He became raucous with his culling sprees, no longer confining himself to Victoria Colony, his designated jurisdiction. There were barely any feral dogs left anyway. Daddy still liked strolling around, terrorizing the creatures in the night.

Sometimes he and I went to an adjacent neighbourhood and bazaar in the middle of the night to shoot, when the clatter of the city had died down and there were no witnesses.

Once he shot a sleeping cat under a chai stall. He said it was an accident.

'Pick it up,' Daddy said when he shot a dog. 'Toss it in that rubbish pile over there.'

Over there. Over here. By that dumpster. By that sewer. In that sewer. In that municipal truck. Just leave it there for other dogs.

The bodies were always warm when I lifted them.

⁂

'You have to deposit the shotgun to the colony administration soon,' Samandar Khan informed Daddy one morning while he and I were hosing down the driveway. The driver watched us and cleaned his ear with the key of the Toyota.

'Why?'

'They'll begin poisoning the dogs from now on,' he said. 'Strychnine in chicken meat. Only the security guards will keep their guns.'

I could see Daddy's face wilt and wither as if he were a little boy and someone was taking away his favourite toy.

'We'll see,' Daddy said. 'I haven't heard of any orders yet.'

'There aren't any dogs left anyway. What will you shoot, sahib ji?'

The two men kept talking. My mind drifted somewhere else, to my own black-and-white dog. How would I save him from poisoned chicken?

'Bad day for you,' Samandar Khan guffawed at Daddy. 'Good day for Nisar Khan, the butcher.'

⁂

With Daddy barely bringing home his salary, a downpour fell upon the family. As months crawled by, Amma had frequent meltdowns. Rashda had not paid her school or evening tuition fee in two months. Like Amma, Rashda often told Daddy to mend his ways. She did not want to work at a call centre like her friend Bushra, or leave her education.

Amma announced that the sir and madam from Bungalow 17 had called her to say they no longer wanted Daddy in the house because of his suspicious habits. They were willing to keep me on as an errand boy and Amma as a new maid, but they did not want my father crossing the threshold.

Suddenly, it was not just the hunting privileges Daddy was losing, but his job at the bungalow too. He had to do other odd jobs to make ends meet. Amma told me I was not allowed in the bungalow kitchen anymore.

'Or their son's bedroom or any other rooms in the house,' she said.

I smelled of cigarettes and other bad things. The family said I smelled like Daddy.

One evening, Amma hollered, wailed, broke two ceramic plates on the kitchen floor, hit her head with her hands in the courtyard, beat her chest and berated Daddy after she found a white powder and syringe in his kameez when she was doing laundry.

Amma held him by the collar and asked why he was hellbent on ruining her life. Daddy pushed her back. She did not fall. I wanted her to. Amma stood steadfast.

Daddy's response was that the cleric at the mosque told him it was the wife who brought good luck and sustenance in a marriage, and that it was Amma who was the manhoos one.

The doomed, unlucky one.

Amma kept spewing curses. Daddy kept spewing them back. I felt I had a duty towards him.

'Leave him alone,' I shouted at Amma. 'If you want more money, go work yourself. Are your arms and legs broken?'

Amma stood, mortified. After a while, she said in a strained voice, 'For two years, I didn't eat lentils because the big pir from Multan told me not to. For years, I prayed for a son. I wouldn't have if I knew this is what he'd become.'

'You shouldn't have prayed, then. You should've strangled me so you could live peacefully with your churail daughter.' Amma did not reply. But I know what she wanted to say.

I wish I had.

⁂

'Do you see how the witches are conspiring against us?' Daddy said to me one night. 'I wish I had more sons who would stand up for their old father.'

'Why did Daniyal's daddy kick you out?'

'Because he is an emasculated son-of-a-bitch who is controlled by his woman. He does what the madam says.'

I reflected and remained quiet.

'How else can a man who is always at the office, never at home, suddenly kick me out of the job?'

There were many other questions I wanted to ask Daddy. Like why did he smoke so much? Smoking kills. Daniyal taught me that phrase. Why did Daddy need an injection? Was he sick? How sick was he? Why couldn't Daddy learn a computer course like Aslam Mamu and get a new job? And a Honda?

Daddy turned to look at me when I did not respond with affirmation. I knew what he was thinking—that I was siding with Amma and betraying him. Before he rebuked me and said his favourite lines—*Why don't you cut your penis and become like Aslam?*—my tongue thawed and I said, 'Why don't we get Rashda married?'

'Marry off your sister?' Daddy considered for a moment. 'This way, she'll be out of the house. Less chitter-chatter. Less drama. Now, you're thinking like a man.'

In the next few days, Daddy was able to convince Amma that my sister would have a better life if she got married to Rehan. She could still sit for her board exams, keep taking science tuitions, and pay for her daily rickshaw rides. It was our cousin's family who would be responsible for her monthly expenditures. Not us. They were better off, anyway.

'It's in the family,' Daddy said. 'What can go wrong? She has to marry after finishing her matriculation anyway, why not a few months earlier? And if you talk to Baji in Bungalow 17, she will help with the dowry.'

Amma thought about it.

'We can have a little ceremony. I know a man who can add a string of lights outside,' he continued. 'I know another man who can put a tent outside for a few guests.'

Amma thought some more.

'My dead grandfather gave my brother his word. We can't break it.'

My sister felt deceived by our mother. She felt Amma was selling her to a man similar to Daddy.

'Why can't I marry a learned man?' she said when the news was broken to her. 'Why can't I marry someone else after matric? A man of my choosing?'

'You've been promised. We gave them our word,' Amma said. 'If we turn our backs on the family, they'll all turn their backs on us. It's also the family's reputation in the village.'

Rashda argued some more, but deep down she knew there was no way out. There had never been a way out for other unhappy family members who wanted to break their arranged betrothals. She became quiet after that decision.

There were times when I tried to engage with her, since I had never seen her so somber, stewing in silence. Whenever she sat in the courtyard with a book in her hands, I could see her eyes straying here and there, everywhere but the words on the paper before her. She almost burnt her hand once trying to boil milk, forgetting where she was and the task she was doing. I did not enjoy this quiet as I thought I would, but Daddy did. Daddy was very happy. After a while, Amma also became happy, once Madam gave her thirty thousand rupees in cash for the dowry. Aslam Mamu was happy to learn we had found a way for Rashda to pass her matric.

I had my own worries. I was dejected by my separation from Daniyal. I was limited to cleaning corridors, the garden and the driveway. The maid had started bringing her son to the bungalow for Daniyal to play with sometimes.

Her son went to school and did not smell of cigarettes.

⁂

A week before the wedding and a few days before Rehan's family and other relatives were to arrive in Lahore from Hafizabad, Rashda went missing. Her charpoy was empty. Her school bag and a few clothes were also gone.

Amma and I looked everywhere. Around the servant quarters. Around Victoria Colony. After a while, we began looking for Daddy. After failing at that too, we resumed the first search. We took a rickshaw to Rashda's school, the tuition centre, and her friend Bushra's house.

My sister was nowhere to be found.

Around noon, two police constables arrived at our house in a rickety blue pickup with blue and red lights on top. They had found the dead, bloody body of a young girl on Canal Road, not far from Victoria Colony. She was hit by a car while attempting to cross the wide road in the middle of the night. The streetlamps were not working due to a short circuit.

They had found her name scribbled on the first page of her school diary, where she had also written down Aslam Mamu's new mobile number. He identified the body at the morgue.

Amma did not cry. She did not shriek. She howled. It was a guttural howl like that of a wounded animal. Like that dog when Daddy shot him only in the leg.

Her cry pierced my skin, penetrated my bones, wrecked something in my heart.

My body went numb. Amma howled again. And again. And again. I wanted to stop her pain. I wanted to strangle Amma to soothe her pain, and then go hunting for Daddy.

⌘

Aslam mamu and I did not speak much as we followed the blaring Edhi ambulance home on his motorbike. My sister was inside that ambulance. I held onto her school bag and clothes as my uncle zoomed through Lahore traffic. We took the same Canal Road home. And the same thirty thousand rupees that Daniyal's mother had handed Amma were to be used on the funeral instead.

As Aslam Mamu and I halted at a red light, I watched the white ambulance. I thought I saw small, flickering fireflies dancing through the car doors, around the windows, the taillights, and the exhaust pipe. My uncle did not react. He could not see. Perhaps it was merely a mirage cast by the streetlight. I remained transfixed by the soft glow of those few fireflies I could catch in the palm of my hand. Escaping. Soaring. Floating in the dusty, dirty, murky air. Up. Up. Into the heavens.

The night after the burial, Daddy went on the prowl again, hunting dogs. He was reeling out of control again. I followed him.

Daddy's mourning was different from Amma's. He swung the shotgun after the mourners left and after my sister was buried in a small graveyard nearby, and he shot everything that night. He told me that he would shoot everything before they could take away his gun.

He shot chickens. Rats.

His kikar tree.

An old discarded glass table in the garbage pile. It shattered everywhere. He shot inside a gutter.

Daddy and I reached the scaffolding near Bungalow 17. A lightbulb hung at the construction site, illuminating only a small area. Everything else rested in the shadows.

I knew my black-and-white dog would not be there. I had not seen him in a while. I expected him to have been poisoned and dumped somewhere by now. A part of me was glad that I didn't see his dead body. I was still unable to erase my sister from my mind. Rashda's body had been draped in a white shroud, and we had carried it to the graveyard, slowly lowered it into a freshly dug grave. I had placed a mound of dirt on her corpse.

I tried to trick Daddy into leaving the scaffolding. I could not see another dead body that day. I told him there was a security guard manning the construction site.

Daddy kept moving forward.

'The security guard has a gun,' I warned.

Daddy stumbled over a brick, regained his balance, and continued walking.

'Did you hear something?' he asked.

Just then, my black-and-white dog emerged at a distance from behind a plastic tarp. He was frailer. I heaved a sigh of relief to see he was alive and breathing.

The dog wagged his tail upon recognizing me, but whined and moved back when he saw Daddy with the shotgun.

'Here'—Daddy handed me the gun. 'You're a man now. Shoot it. See how it feels.'

I locked eyes with Daddy. His eyes were tinged with red. 'No, Daddy.'

He loaded the barrel of the shotgun and shoved the gun into my arms again. I shoved it back.

'Daddy. No. Don't,' I shook my head violently. 'We can't.'

Daddy pushed me away and aimed for the dog. I tugged at Daddy's arm, wrestling him for the gun. He pushed me away with great force and I fell to the ground. Daddy aimed the shotgun at me. I did not cower or raise my hands in surrender as I had seen actors do in the movies I watched with Daniyal. My hands, touching the ground, quivered a little from dread, from disbelief. What would Daddy do in that moment? What would he do if I moved? What would he do if I stayed still?

I restrained myself from getting up.

I looked straight at Daddy. I looked into his eyes. There was nothing there. Nothing. There was no splinter of emotion to be found.

Daddy chuckled, shaking his head, delighted that he had frightened me. He turned the shotgun towards the dog. I looked away because I knew what was coming. I did not cover my ears. There was a loud ringing in my ears from the gunshot.

From the corner of my eye, I saw something move. Fireflies. Thousands of them. Glowing. Gliding. Hovering above the black-and-white dog's body. Wafting through the old ghostly trees. Away from Victoria Colony. Away from Daddy.

I walked home in silence, leaving Daddy by himself.

When Daddy returned home eventually, he told me he had shot many other things after I left him. I squatted on the floor and looked up at Daddy, who was sitting on the charpoy in the courtyard, cleaning the shotgun with a rag. His face, weathering after years and years of sitting behind the kikar tree, suddenly looked sinister to me. His blackened lips. His stained, yellow teeth. The deep pockmarks on his cheek. His balding brown head. Everything about him was grotesque. My heart was laced with an unfamiliar, foreign feeling for the aging man—violent abhorrence.

He said he would return the gun tomorrow. He continued cleaning in hushed silence.

I wanted the gun to go off, for one of the slugs to ricochet and kill Daddy. He broke my heart. He broke Amma's heart. He broke Rashda.

'Sister-fucker,' I whispered.

'What did you say?'

'If someone kills you and throws your body in a gutter,' I said, 'no one will come looking for you. No one will miss you, Daddy.'

I said he was a stray, feral, useless thing no one wanted. 'Haraam-khor,' Daddy abused me, enraged. 'Unfaithful. Coward.'

'I don't want to be like you.'

'Haraam-khor.'

Haraam-khor. Haraam-khor.

Daddy kept chanting as I left him in the courtyard.

Carry It All

She dreamt of fire again. Of things catching fire. The old house. The big garden. The elementary school down the road. Her dead twin's face and hair. She dreamt of flames of red, orange and blue, eating the dressing table and melting the turquoise wallpaper. Grey smoke, thick and billowing out the windows and into the air, choking her sister, squeezing her lungs.

When Aisha woke up, she was sweating. Her breath rasped in her throat. She took a sip from the water on her bedside table, placed a hand over her chest to feel her pounding heart, then cradled her belly to soothe the baby. It was little, but it was there. The doctor had said so. She was twelve weeks along. Missing her period was a normal thing, had been since she was thirteen. Now she was thirty-four. She dismissed it when she did not bleed for three months, thinking it was nothing, until Dr Salma confirmed that she was expecting for the fourth time.

Aisha did not know what to make of the news, whether to rejoice or worry. The babies did not stay inside her. They dissolved, slipped to wherever dead babies go. A heavenly orphanage for ghostly, unborn children. Into a crevice in the skies. A realm somewhere. The limbo. After a while, Aisha stopped wondering where.

Her husband Yasir slept next to her in bed. He snored and drooled on the new pillow cover, dreaming of things, she assumed, other than fire. She gave him a long, sulky look. He had always been a heavy sleeper. She would have to wait until the next day to tell him about the dream. In these odd times, she wished her father-in-law were still alive. The two had been friends. And in his peculiar way he listened—sitting in the living room with a book in his lap, glasses perched on the edge of his nose, nodding along thoughtfully as she went on and on about her nightmares and heartaches and good college days. He made her feel seen and reminded her that she was still a whole person even if motherhood was not in her destiny.

But it had to be in her destiny, she would think. If she were to keep Yasir.

Her father-in-law's funeral was the second one where she had collapsed and broken down. Since then, she hadn't spoken of her nightmares to anyone; she buried them. Tucked them away like the pleats of her dupatta.

Aisha flipped the switch on her lamp, but still it remained dark. The power was out. Her cotton kameez clung to her damp back. She had not noticed the silence or the heat before, but now the room felt too still without the whirring of the ceiling fan or the humming of the air conditioner. She walked to the glass window that overlooked the garden, pushed back the sheer curtains, and slid it open. A splendid gust of wind blew into the burning room and engulfed her as she stood, her hands clasped over her belly, looking at the dark foliage of trees.

From her spot by the window, she could see the rows of money plants in the corner of the garden, a special request she had asked of the gardener. Her mother-in-law said that a money plant brought luck into lives, marriages and bodies. Aisha needed it all. She needed all the money plants in the world.

After a while, the cooling wind turned chilly and Aisha stepped away from the window and slipped back into bed. As they always did when her mind was idle, her thoughts drifted to her sister, Kamila—the first funeral where she had broken down.

Growing up, no one could tell Kamila and Aisha apart. They had the same dark eyes and hair, and smooth and luminous skin. They were both shy, gentle, and gullible. The only difference between them was their bodies. Kamila bled each month. Aisha did not.

When they were eight, they would climb the old peepal tree in their backyard. The rough bark scratched their knees and palms as they ascended. They pretended they had a house up there nestled in the branches and that the green heartshaped leaves were curtains sheltering their little world. They pretended their imaginary husbands were away for work, leaving them to cook and whisper in their leafy sanctuary. When the husbands returned, they smiled and were loved in returned.

And then the girls grew up.

Adulthood shattered the mirrors of their dreams. As far away as the peepal tree's branches were from the ground, so was the reality when they got married. They discovered soon enough that marriages are difficult. Houses could not always become homes. And real husbands could not always be appeased with smiles and good meals. In the real world—bodies mattered, and in some houses, fertility was the only currency.

Three years ago, Kamila had doused herself in gasoline and set herself on fire after a row with her husband. It was a bad marriage. She wanted to leave but could not. Her husband had warned that if she left, she would have nothing to support the children, even if the court granted her custody as their mother. Kamila had no money or savings to raise them, since her husband had forced her to quit her job when they married. He said it was his responsibility to earn for the family, not hers.

For months after Kamila's death, there were nights Aisha felt a sudden wave of sharp pain in her chest, as if someone were punching her, pushing her, trying to reach in through her ribs and pull out her heart. In those moments, she felt Kamila's presence, felt her through the grief. The grief that would never escape her. The grief that festered in silence.

Eventually, Kamila's presence made way for her ghost. A spectral presence. Aisha saw her, saw her figure, lurking, following. Kamila visited in her sister's dreams, drifted through the hallways of the house, a large and drafty building in an affluent neighbourhood. Aisha and Yasir had shared the space with his parents, but now, with his father gone and no extra people around, the house felt even vaster. Kamila managed to find Aisha in the vastness: in the garden, in the bedrooms, in her own reflection in the bathroom mirror. The same eyes, mouth and hair. The same face staring back. It appeared, its mouth agape as if struggling to speak. But the ghost had no voice. And Aisha never understood the strange, strained lip movements, or the intentions behind her sister's piercing eyes. Aisha, on her back, stared up at the ceiling. Sometimes she pretended she was Kamila. Kamila, still moving, doing the dishes. Kamila, still breathing, walking in the garden.

Kamila, still alive, on her back, staring up at the ceiling.

Aisha lay prone, breathing in and out slowly, trying to escape herself and become her sister. In the darkness, she almost succeeded. But suddenly, the room came alive. The lamp turned on and showered the room in a soft glow. The fan whirred and the air conditioner started humming, a loud, incessant drone. And the air itself. Something felt different.

Panicked, Aisha looked down and saw drops of blood on the bedroom floor. A trail of spots that started from the foot of the bed and ended by the window. She swiftly sat up and pulled the sheets from her legs. Her shalwar and the cotton bedsheet were stained red.

'Ya Allah!' she cried in a hushed voice, careful not to wake her sleeping husband.

She rose and yanked the bedsheet from underneath her body. The blood had penetrated deep inside the mattress.

She knew what it was.

She knew what had happened.

She did not want to say it out loud.

How is this possible? she asked herself, frantic. There was nothing this time: no abdominal cramp, no announcement of any kind. Just a dream, and then blood, more blood.

She hadn't even felt it. The baby had quietly left her body, unceremoniously fled her womb, and rejected her as a mother.

Her body was a home to no one.

Nothing.

Not anymore.

Aisha hastily turned off the lamp, then drew back the curtains so the light from the garden could illuminate the room. Yasir and his mother could not know. They would never know. She had to clean the mess.

She always remembered the first time she had lost a baby. It was the night of Kamila's funeral, when the pain of one loss blended with the raw sadness of another, melting sorrow in her bones and body.

Aisha often wondered if the next miscarriages occurred because of the strange dreams, or because of Kamila's ghost, who refused to leave her alone, or because of the anger she felt towards Kamila for abandoning her, or because of her incompetent cervix, which Dr Salma had explained during one of their sessions. From her drawer she had pulled out a pamphlet and a red ballpoint pen and pointed to a uterus shaped like a mango, a baby with an umbilical cord floating inside. This was the closest Aisha had come to seeing a full-term baby inside her womb. It was a beautiful picture. She had saved it. Pulled it out of the notepad, folded it and put it in her Michael Kors bag—a gift from Yasir when he had found out she was pregnant the second time. There had been hope then. He had taken her out for dinner.

After a couple more tries, Dr Salma no longer drew pictures of babies and wombs. Instead, she suggested alternatives. 'There's also IVF ...'

'I don't know. I don't know,' replied Aisha. 'I'll have to speak with Yasir.'

But she did not want to speak with Yasir, who would in turn speak to his mother. Yasir knew kindness; his mother did not. Following the third baby, Yasir's mother finally said what had been living in her mind for months. 'Losing babies should not be a constant thing. It should not become the norm. If it is, then we have a problem, Yasir. Don't you think it's a problem?'

Aisha remembered smoking a cigarette in the guest bathroom that night. Her hands had trembled, her body had shivered, a little from anger but much more from anxiety. The cigarette was an act of defiance, a temporary escape. Yasir hated women who smoked. Aisha herself felt like a burning candle: her body, too, was depleting fast, wax dripped slowly and quietly on the floor.

Yasir and his mother worried about who the family business would go to if there were no children. Yasir was the only son. His mother often joked that Yasir could always bring in a new bride. A newer, younger, fertile bride, to do what was necessary. Yasir never offered a reply. He never said a thing.

While Yasir's family was busy placing all the blame on her, Aisha wondered if it was in fact her mother-in-law's venom and her husband's passiveness that had killed the third baby, who refused to be born into such a family. Sometimes she was certain that it was what had happened.

⁂

Aisha was still bleeding on the bed. Warm blood trickled down her legs, but before rushing to the bathroom to wash herself, she ran her fingers over the bedsheet. Her trembling fingers scavenged through each fold and crevice in the sheet looking for the lost thing.

A clot. A tissue. A piece of flesh. A baby. *Her* baby.

What does it look like?

She found it, and it was small. Unborn. Quiet. So still. It fit in the corner of her palm. It looked nothing like the baby in Dr Salma's picture, or the photos she had looked at on Google, or the colourful pictures inside the baby books she collected. Every time, she looked for the remnants. But this was the first time she had seen what she kept losing. She had never been this far along before.

She brought it close to her ear.

Is the heart beating? Is it there?

It was not.

She caressed it with her thumb. It was translucent, pink and blue, and soft like velvet.

Aisha put her baby on a facial tissue on her bedside table and delayed her mourning for later. Fear gripped her more tightly than grief.

She had to clean everything up first. That was more important.

She locked the bedroom door and rushed into the bathroom. She tossed her blood-soaked shalwar in the tub and put on clean trousers, underwear and two sanitary pads. The blood had also stained the back of her kameez. She would change that later.

Aisha returned to the bedroom and squatted down to scrub the hard tiles with a towel and hot water. The bed was a mess. She wanted to burn it, and then herself. She looked for a clean bedsheet in the closet. She felt feverish and dizzy but still she pressed on, muttering to herself quietly.

She did not have to tell anyone about the baby, she decided. She could play a game. She could go to the baby shower her sister-in-law was planning. She could continue to let Yasir's mother pray over her belly. She could keep seeing Dr Salma. She could pay the doctor for her silence. And when the time came, she could kill herself, throw herself off the balcony, or set herself on fire like Kamila. They had always been similar. They could die the same way.

Aisha carefully tried to peel the bedsheet from under Yasir. She gently tugged. He stirred and shifted slightly; a soft sigh escaped his lips. With each careful pull, she worked the sheets free. The fabric whispered. His legs moved.

'Hmm?' A furrow formed on his brow. His eyes still closed.

'Just a minute,' she said as she slipped the sheet free. 'I spilled some water.'

She looked down at him sleeping serenely. She loathed him in that moment. That was his whole existence. Serenity. Everything in that house moved around his survival and comfort. Everything was designed for him by his mother. After Yasir graduated with his business degree, his father had hired him at his real estate company. His mother had found him a beautiful bride. And since this bride could not bear children, she was going to find him another. It was as easy as that.

'There's a reason Islam allows four marriages,' Aisha once overheard her mother-in-law telling Yasir.

'Hmm,' he replied.

Later, when Aisha and Yasir were alone, she confronted him. 'I'm not an old car or piece of furniture that you can replace and upgrade!'

'Hmm,' he replied.

Aisha kept looking down at Yasir. She hated everything about him. His hands. His arms. That mole on his cheek. The big house. The big garden. The big car. The serene, fireless slumber. She wanted to smother him in his sleep. Break a money plant pot over his head and escape.

No, not escape, she thought, but stand there by his body so his mother could see his lifeless form when she pushed open their bedroom door in the morning to wake them up.

Aisha washed the stains in the mattress with a mixture of cold water and shampoo. Then, she put a new bedsheet on her side of the bed and underneath Yasir in such a way that he would think that it had slipped from beneath him when he turned in his sleep.

She lifted the baby from the bedside table and rushed to the garden, barefoot, running on tiptoes to avoid being heard.

In the emptiness of the garden, she looked around at the dark trees.

Where should the grave be?

Somewhere soft. Somewhere warm.

She settled on a flower pot, small and uninhabited, a protected space. As her fingers dug the little grave, she finally wept.

How big should the grave be? Small. Very small. Even still, it was too much work. Her body gave up, and she collapsed on the grass. Her eyes fixed on the dark skies, her body motionless and still. She felt she was falling, falling into a well, into fire, into a dark, empty womb.

In burying the baby, she would bury the last part of herself. Who was she? Merely a pile of ash. A shadow in a big house. That deadened brown leaf in the money plant. Yasir's infertile wife. A dead sister's reflection.

The stillness, the quiet of the hushed night was broken by the sound of rustling. There was rustling in the garden. Aisha kept low to the ground, watching the leaves of the neem tree move in the windless night, as if stirred awake by a restless spirit. Unfazed, unperturbed, Aisha closed her eyes. She knew what was coming, who was coming for her.

She took a deep breath and surrendered to the moment. No longer fighting it. No longer hiding from her shadow. Her limbs loosened, relaxing for the first time in years. For a very long time, she had felt as though her body were on fire, that there was a vehement, relentless blaze raging beneath her skin, scorching every vessel, every fibre, every nerve. Now someone had poured cold water on her. The wind drew closer. She kept a hand on her belly. There was a sudden rush of air near her face.

She had found Aisha. Kamila's ghost.

Aisha gently opened her eyes and looked up at her sister's silhouette. Moonlight streaked through the ghost's hair, her fingers, her hips. Aisha felt Kamila's presence all around her. She could almost feel her breath on her ear. She could almost feel her body heat. She pictured Kamila in her last days. So frail. So lean. So morbidly unhappy. So terrifyingly loud at times, and so depressingly numb at others.

Kamila bent down and whispered something in Aisha's ear. Aisha leaned in, desperate for her sister, desperate for some relief, desperate for answers. For the first time, she could hear her sister's words clearly. They unfurled inside Aisha's mind and body.

'Yes, you're right,' Aisha whispered back to Kamila. 'You're absolutely right. I will. We will.'

And then, there was black.

⌘

When Aisha woke up, dawn was breaking, and the baby was already buried in a potted grave. She peeled herself off the ground and walked back to the house. The maids would be arriving soon. The gardener would ring the bell to rouse the family.

Aisha carried everything back with her to the bedroom: the ghost, the empty belly, the absence, the blood, the shortness of breath, the chills, the pallor, the secret and the sunless sky.

When she returned, Yasir was sitting on the bed, groggy-eyed. His hair was the only messy thing in the spotless room. 'Where did you go?' he asked. 'Did you go to get more water from the kitchen?'

Aisha quietly turned around and began to fish for a new kameez from the closet. Yasir's eyes went straight to the bloodstain, which Aisha hadn't had time to wash out. The bright red had dulled into russet brown.

'What happened?'

Aisha opened her mouth to answer but could not. She was exhausted. Burnt. Gone. He was not worth answering.

'What happened?' he asked for the second time, anxiously.

'A murder,' she replied. 'Your mother killed me four years ago when she chose me for you,' she replied.

'What?'

'I was a teacher before I met you, and I was happy.'

Yasir looked perplexed. 'What? What are you saying? What do you mean?'

'I liked your father. I wish he hadn't left us so soon,' she said softly.

His eyes widened and his lips parted as he searched for clarity. 'What?'

'You told me you could make me happier.' She sat on the bed. 'My mother told me this big house would make me happier. Your mother told me being your wife was a privilege and it would make me happier. The world told me being a mother would make me happier. But it's been a joke. Everything with you has been a big, bloody joke.'

Yasir's eyebrows knit together in confusion. His mouth was open. Aisha could tell that he was struggling to find words, something unsavoury that could pierce her skin, shake her, make her tremble. A torrent of words that could tear through her body and make her doubt or regret what she had said, only to have him comfort her later, after he had made it all her fault. He did that often.

'I'm leaving you. I'm leaving this house.'

She got up from the bed and looked at herself in the bedroom mirror. Tired eyes. Flecks of grey in her hair. She was only in her thirties. She had aged sooner than she was supposed to. She wanted to shower with hot water, wash the blood off herself, wash the stained shalwar, the bedsheet, watch the fabrics cling tightly to her chest as she rinsed herself. She wanted to free herself. Free herself of everything.

Yasir stood up, asking her to relax and talk to him. Telling her that what she was saying was stupid and nonsensical.

That she shouldn't leave. He took a few steps towards her, still fumbling through his words, dumbly scratching his balding head, trying to process the situation. How Aisha could leave so easily. He made a small guttural noise as if to speak, but before the words could leave his lips, a burst of light appeared near the window.

The bedroom curtain was on fire. Aisha took a few steps back, shocked. Flames, out of nowhere, licked the sheer, delicate fabric, catching quickly and shooting up the walls. Yasir flailed around, suspended in disbelief for a moment before regaining his senses and rushing to hold a pillow to the curtain, trying to smother the consuming flames. He screamed. 'Fire! Fire!' He tried to tear the blazing curtain down, but the flames were too hot.

Aisha remained frozen. Gripped at first by fear, though that feeling soon gave way to something else. Something warmer. Something lovely. As she watched the fire snake around the room, catching on the bed, the rug, the dresser, her discarded clothes, she felt peace. Embraced by the orange and yellow glow. Understood.

'Come on!' Yasir was desperate now. 'Help me, Aisha!' She didn't. She didn't care. About the fire. About his screams. About him. She giggled, and then the giggles turned into full-throated laughter. Yasir, who was now at the door, looked back at her in shock. She put her hand over her mouth to smother her wide-stretched smile. There should be some shame.

'The door is jammed,' he said. 'It won't open. It won't open!'

Aisha wondered if she had locked the door when she stepped inside. She did not recall.

'Help! Help!' Yasir yelled, coughing between words. Smoke billowed around them as the fire's orange tendrils crawled around the ceiling. There was now a strong scent of burning fabric and ash. This was all too much for Yasir. He crumpled to the ground, gagging uncontrollably. He reached out his hand to Aisha. She looked down at her husband, a man who had never extended a helping hand when she trembled. She observed him as a curious cat might observe a fly, ensnared in a spider's web.

The flames were at her feet. But she did not feel them. She did not feel anything. She looked towards the door. Amidst the blurry frenzy, through fiery fingers, Aisha could just make out the shape of a figure. A shadow, moving slowly across the room. As it came towards her, Aisha saw her dark eyes and dark hair reflected back at her.

She held out her hand. Her sister did the same. Aisha swore she could feel a set of fingertips touching her own. The smoke was overpowering now, the flames bright and towering. Yet Aisha stood standing. She stood standing until her vision began to fade, until her muscles gave way, until she fell softly into her sister's loving embrace. And in that moment, she understood her sister perfectly. She understood Kamila's words, her struggles, the tests, the failures, the burden. And just like that, the weight she hadn't even named began to lift.

The Last Days of Bilquees Begum

She had come home to die. And I had arrived to make the last days easier. My job, as it was described by the friend who had referred me, would be to take care of her until the end.

When I saw Bilquees Begum for the first time, she was lying on a big rosewood bed which she had brought with her thirty-two years ago in her dowry. She was frail and grim, like a small delicate bird tucked in a muddled nest of blankets, medicine, water bottles, blood pressure apparatus and an oxygen cylinder. Her eyes were closed and her mouth slightly open. A yellow cotton kameez with green embroidered flowers fell off her bony shoulders.

She was not dead yet, just asleep. But there was nothing peaceful in that slumber. Life escaped in every breath, snore, and sputter.

'Do you know why you have been called here?' her husband, Muhammad Rauf, asked me.

I stood in the kitchen watching the maid, Ghazala, stir chicken broth on the stove for the sick woman.

I nodded. Muhammad Rauf stared.

He was a religious man with a group of religious friends who often paid visits to the house. According to Muhammad Rauf and the big mufti, there was an evil shadow, a sinister ghost, hovering in the rooms, wrecking the lives of the residents within. Muhammad Rauf had lost huge sums of money in his garment business. Bilquees Begum became very unwell a few months afterwards and the medical bills had started to pile up. It was all the shadow's evildoing.

My eyes trailed from Muhammad Rauf's long, coarse, greying beard to his black turban, before landing on the marble chip floor.

'My wife is dying,' he said in a sober voice. 'Cancer. She cannot move much, and needs round-the-clock care.'

There was no sentiment in his voice—a sign that he had explained the situation many times to different people, and to himself. It was just a thing that was happening now. A devastating, inevitable piece of reality he could not pray away.

His wife was dying.

It was that simple.

Then, out of nowhere, he asked, 'Muslim?'

I did not want to answer that heavy question but dutifully and quietly whispered, 'No, Christian.'

Deep wrinkles populated his forehead. I watched as his mind seemed to wrestle with the conflict between faith and desperation. It was the desperate need of a desperate hour.

To allow a Christian girl to cook food, touch, feed, bathe and clothe his pious Muslim wife in her last days.

Five caretakers had already vacated the annexe. Given up and left. Ghazala told me that they had found the man of the house too formidable, too temperamental. A few had even stolen from the family while Bilquees Begum was asleep and Muhammad Rauf was out praying at the mosque. Good blankets which Bilquees had stitched when she was younger. Silver cutlery. China. Bedsheets. Small kitchen appliances. A toaster and a sandwich maker. A gold bangle from Bilquees's wrist. Her frayed wedding clothes.

'Noorie,' Muhammad Rauf pondered as we stood in the kitchen. 'I thought Noorie was a Muslim name.'

I did not reply.

'Now that I think about it, you do look like a Christian.' He said Muslims had a glow about them. An aura. A pure, divine, celestial glow that coated their faces and bodies. There was no glow in me. And I was too dark-skinned to be a Muslim anyway. A Christian or a Hindu perhaps, but not a Muslim, he echoed.

'I'll take care of everything,' I assured Muhammad Rauf. 'I worked at the house of another woman who had her lymph nodes removed. She was in deep pain.'

I remembered massaging that woman's shoulders, chest and arms when they swelled. I had also looked after a woman who had dementia and who thought a pillow was her newborn baby. And a sickly child who had leukemia. I did not tell him that they all died. Through no fault of my own.

'You didn't finish nursing school, did you?' he asked. 'Couldn't,' I shook my head.

He paused to reflect.

'Bedsores. Diapers. Medicines. Massage. Chicken broth. Stories,' I said. 'You can trust me with your wife.'

'Alright,' he said after much consideration. 'You'll be her caretaker. There's a room on the rooftop. You'll sleep there.'

It was June and it was hot up in the allotted room. I was given a charpoy, a pedestal fan, a wooden cupboard for my belongings and a tap of running water outside. At nighttime, a flickering white tube light attracted lizards, moths and mosquitoes. The moths longed for the glimmer of the tube light. The lizards longed for the moths. The mosquitoes longed for my blood. And I, in that stirring, withering Lahore heat, longed for an air conditioner and a better life. A life where my father was still moving and working. A life where I was still at college, spending weekends eating orange-flavoured ice candy in the park with friends. And a life where there was money for the bills, and my mother did not have to scrub other people's toilet bowls and shower cabins.

The reality was bleakly simple: I needed Bilquees Begum as much as she needed me.

⁂

I had taken a bus from Sialkot to Lahore to become a nursemaid. Thirty thousand rupees per month.

I was twenty. I had abandoned nursing school after my father had a stroke the prior year. He had become somewhat like Bilquees Begum—merely existing on a mattress with his eyes fixed on the flaking walls of our three-room quarter. Waiting to be changed. Waiting to die. Being the oldest child, I had to become the provider for the household. To do what my father could not.

Soon after my father's sickness, Mother began cleaning people's bathrooms and verandas to make ends meet, and I started taking care of others for a living. The woman with dementia, the sickly child. All good jobs that did not last. When a friend heard about a job seeking a caretaker for Bilquees Begum, we decided it was too good an opportunity to ignore.

'We must save every rupee now, Noorie, at least for a while,' Mother said to me before I left for Lahore. I promised to obey but betrayed that promise almost as soon as I arrived at the bus station.

There, I found a curious old man in a brown shalwar kameez sitting cross-legged on a bamboo mat with white envelopes sprawled lazily before him. Next to him was a birdcage which housed a bright green parrot with a red beak. There was a sign on the floor promising to reveal the future, for a price. I couldn't resist giving the man fifty rupees to tell my fortune.

'Hundred rupees for a good one,' he winked.

I shook my head and thrust a fifty-rupee note into his ashy palm. He gave me a low salute and put it into his pocket. He let the parrot out of its cage, a dingy thing lined with bird waste, pearl millet grain and a newspaper clipping about how a prominent politician running for election had a secret wife who was also a famous stage dancer, claiming it was his religious right.

'Tell the girl the truth,' the old man said to the parrot, stroking its head.

Yes, tell the girl the truth, I thought. The thought was more like a prayer.

The parrot walked around the envelopes, bobbing its little head up and down, taking small steps over the floor of white paper before picking one. The old man handed the selected envelope to me.

I turned it over in my hand once or twice, as if trying to read the fortune through the closed envelope. For a moment, I was worried I had wasted my money. I wasn't sure I really wanted to know what was inside. Before I could think too much, a vendor wheeling a cart of old scraps—newspapers, notebooks, boxes, telephones and useless kitchen appliances—asked me to get out of his way so he could park. I moved to the side of the pavement and opened the envelope. I glanced at the fortune that I had wasted fifty rupees on and frowned, unable to decipher the meaning of the words on the page, or how they in any way related to my life. I slid the paper in my wallet, dropping the empty envelope on the ground, and left the old man and his parrot to read the fortunes of other wearied souls.

⁂

Bilquees Begum's chemo treatment stopped four months before I began working for her, and since that time she had slowly descended into a vegetative state. She was supposed to have died years ago, when the stage four breast cancer was first diagnosed. But her body did not surrender. The spirit remained unbroken. She saw many winters, saw all her children married, painted the whole house, and helped her husband in his business.

'She hid it for so long,' Ghazala told me. She had worked for the family for over three years. 'The cancer. She didn't want to take off her kameez and be naked in front of a doctor. She found it to be shameful.'

I watched Ghazala prepare a Rooh Afza drink for Feroze, the young nurse who had just passed by to enter Bilquees's room. She twisted the white cap from the tall bottle and I watched the red syrup drip into the glass. She poured cool water from the jug and asked me to stir the solution with a spoon.

Feroze paid a visit every few days for Bilquees Begum's IV drip. It was becoming harder to make her eat or move. Her body needed protein.

'You know what happens in cancer?' Ghazala said. 'A lump in this area …'

She pulled her dupatta to the side and discreetly pointed at her breasts beneath her shirt. I knew what she was saying, but I humoured her as she described Bilquees Begum's medical history as if she were a doctor.

'Then, two years ago, she was clear.' Ghazala stirred the chicken curry on the stove.

'So she did start seeing a doctor?' I asked.

'Oh yes, she had to,' Ghazala said. 'She shrunk. Her family pushed her to.'

I chopped coriander leaves and onions for the garnish. Ghazala told me to hand her the canister that contained rice. Muhammad Rauf preferred rice over roti.

'The hospital told her to remove the …' She pointed at her chest. 'Chop them off in a surgery, in case the cancer returns. But she was determined not to.'

I peered over the counter and looked at Bilquees Begum resting on her bed. Feroze was setting up a glucose drip. He looked at me and smiled. I smiled back coyly.

'What is a woman without the God-gifted female organs?' Ghazala said. 'I know another woman who lives around the corner. The doctor says there is a tumour in her ovaries. She can't bear children but she refuses the surgery in case she miraculously bears one.'

I was distracted by Feroze. I accidentally cut my finger with the knife and watched as drops of blood fell on the wooden board. I put the cut finger in my mouth and sucked lightly to soothe the sharp pain.

Ghazala shook her head, disappointed at my negligence. She wrapped a corner of her dupatta around my finger to apply pressure to the cut.

'These things make a woman, you know. Breasts, ovaries, cooking, housekeeping, moving around her house.' Ghazala gently pressed my covered finger. 'Without them, she's an empty vessel. The woman is an empty thing.'

Ghazala looked at me and then at Feroze, who was now packing up his medical bag, preparing to leave. She asked me to get a Band-Aid from him and to hand him the Rooh Afza drink.

'If your attention keeps straying, many other things will be cut from your life, Noorie Begum,' Ghazala rebuked me. 'Don't forget why you're here.'

In the murky room upstairs with the fan and the whirring white tube light and the creaking insects, I took off my paisley kameez and examined my breasts in a small hand mirror swiped from Bilquees Begum's bedroom. I ran my hands slowly over my flesh, embarrassed by the intimacy of the act. I saw no lumps, felt no lumps.

I don't bleed more than normal.

I don't bleed less than normal.

I didn't want to die like Bilquees Begum. Hung before servants and family members as a sad spectacle.

Muhammad Rauf spent many hours in his wife's room, sitting on a prayer rug, nursing her and reciting verses from the Quran. Her children, too, visited often with their young ones.

'So you've come to see me rot,' Bilquees said to me one day as I entered her bedroom. She had said this to me before, variations of the same phrase, but never remembered them the next day.

Often she told me not to see her naked. Not to touch her soiled diaper and urine mat. Her husband could change her. Her husband *should* change her. Every time I responded that he had gone to the mosque to pray. These were the words he gave me, which I in turn relayed. I could not leave her dirty. I could not leave her vulnerable to infection.

'Do you have lice in your hair?' she had said to me as I changed her into a new pair of shalwar. 'The previous maid gave me lice.'

I'm not a maid. I'm a nurse. I'm a caretaker.

There were lapses in Bilquees Begum's time and memory. Her voice was dim.

I just smiled and shook my head no.

'It's Friday today,' she said on a Tuesday.

'It's twelve in the afternoon now,' she said once at 3 a.m. That night she had refused to sleep. Her body jolted and itched all over. She asked me to put her in the wheelchair and roll her into the kitchen.

It was difficult, not because she was heavy, but because she was fragile, breakable, like the stained-glass jug she made me dust with a rag and put on the top shelf in the dining room.

Her body might have been shutting down piece by piece, becoming something she could no longer control, but she was still very much in love with her house and mourned the items that had been stolen.

I cleaned and rearranged all the glasses, dinner plates, and steel spoons on the shelves and in the drawers upon her hoarse, strained commands. She knew every nook and cranny of the house. At times I could see, in her, sweet glimpses of a woman who had once bought land with her husband and built a house she ruled, vivid residues of her former self like bright ambers.

Everywhere I went I noticed glass bottles sitting on shelves and tables. Old, fancy, empty, expensive alcohol vessels she had collected for decoration from flea markets over the years.

⌘

Although they possessed a strange beauty, it was curious for one house to have so many bottles. In the bedroom. In the kitchen. Lined up on a sunlit shelf in the bathroom. A bedazzled Chivas Regal had a dead money plant in dirty water. Smirnoff vodka had a string of unlit fairy lights. Johnnie Walker Black Label housed mustard oil for hair and body. Other bottles held ground spices, ribbons, buttons, marbles. Something was always inside the bottles. They were rarely empty.

Ghazala said the bottles had not always been so full. It was only after Bilquees's chemo stopped that she had started filling the glass, and assigned the previous caretaker the duty of coming up with things to store in the bottles.

Bilquees Begum did not like looking at empty bottles.

I found it amusing to watch Muhammad Rauf and the big mufti walk around the house ignoring the filled bottles and what they meant, pacing in their Peshawari chappals, wooden rosaries in hand.

⁂

When Bilquees Begum had the rare strength and a clear mind, sometimes for a few minutes and occasionally for hours on a good day, she talked to me often. She had to. I was the only company available for long, dreary hours.

Between the chicken broth and spittle, between shampooing the wisps of her pixie grey hair, while I massaged her skeletal legs, we conversed about my family and hers, her selected memories and mine.

'Do you also think this house is haunted?' Bilquees Begum asked me one day.

I was clipping her toenails. Ghazala overheard the question as she entered the room carrying a glass of warm milk for Bilquees Begum. She let out a small breath, absorbing the stupidity of the question, the corners of her mouth twitching as she fought back a smile. She placed the milk on the side table and tapped her temple, followed by a dismissive wave. I knew instantly what she meant. She wanted me to ignore Bilquees Begum.

Ghazala believed she had gone mad.

'I've not seen anything,' I replied to Bilquees Begum, looking away from Ghazala, who was now leaving.

'Hmm?'

'I've not seen anything.'

'Rauf says he often sees a shadow following me around the house. Do you see it too?'

I stopped clipping and leaned back, surveying the white walls in the bedroom.

'No, no shadow, ghost, or spirit,' I said confidently. 'It's just you in this bed.'

'What about you, up in that dark room by yourself?' she asked. 'Have you ever felt a presence there? Up there in that darkness?'

'No. No presence,' I said. 'No ghosts visit me up there. Only lizards and cockroaches.'

'Do you think Muhammad Rauf and Mufti Nawaz are making a fool out of me, then?'

I looked up at her, not knowing what she meant by that.

She continued speaking in a bleak voice.

'Mufti Sahab visits every week. Do you see that? And each time he tries to convince me to let Muhammad Rauf bring in a besahara, a helpless orphan woman, as a second wife.'

An uneasy silence followed that deeply disconcerting confession.

'A second wife?'

'You see, the men in the mosque think the house is falling apart. It is burning, plunging, because it lacks the presence of a woman. A full woman.'

She motioned to me to massage her aching legs. I pressed my thumbs into her wrinkly skin, making half circles as she cried out in pain, asking me to be gentle.

After a moment, she resumed, 'They say my husband's good deed of giving some poor woman shelter will diminish my pain, bring wealth to this burning house, and help us get rid of the evil ghost. The mufti tells me to think about my husband's welfare. He's been taking care of me for years. He needs someone alive, healthy and wifely to take care of him too, after I'm gone.'

'If you ask me,' I said, 'it's strange to make such preparations while you're still alive.'

'They think it's strange not to.'

I looked at her, disturbed, waiting for her to say something else, as I had nothing to offer in reply.

Bilquees Begum read my troubled face.

'You told me about your father,' she said. 'What does his illness make you feel?'

I was silent for a moment.

'Deeply unhappy. Confused. Sometimes I wish I had a brother who could take care of the family and leave me to my studies.'

'Deeply unhappy,' she repeated. 'But here you are, sitting, moving, working, making money, living. Women can do that. They can survive in burning buildings. Their minds and bodies can remain unscathed.'

She said she believed that men were not built from the same clay as women. Rarely could they weather strong winds and rainstorms.

'Have you ever seen a young widow with children?' she asked. 'She can live many years, garner strength, do many jobs, raise children, marry them off, but a widowed man rarely stays a widowed man. He either becomes a groom again or withers away from a broken heart. Dies early.'

'There must be good men,' I said. 'There must be strong men.'

'There are,' she said. 'I knew one.'

I raised my eyebrows. She beckoned me to come closer to her.

'I've an unfinished thing to do.'

'An unfinished thing?' I asked.

'I want you to help me catch the ghost.'

I looked at Bilquees Begum with suspicion. She was still a stranger to me. A wilting stranger. A decaying stranger, unmoored, ensnared by aching limbs, raspy breaths and bizarre confessions.

'I've known him for years. He has haunted me for years.'

A few slow days went by, during which I did as Bilquees Begum instructed.

I was asked to empty all the decorative bottles around the house. We were going to trap the ghost in a bottle and seal it. And so I went around the house in the afternoons after Muhammad Rauf had gone to the mosque for Asr prayer, while Ghazala sat on the cool marble floor under the ceiling fan in the living room, sipping chai. She watched me tap the backs of brandy and wine bottles, struggling to remove lodged marbles and seashells. She would shake her head, confused about whose odd commands I was following. Certainly not those of a dying woman who was losing touch with life. I told Ghazala once, when she joked about Bilquees Begum's blurring mind and memory, that the old woman was still aware of the world around her, that she was not just lying in a bedroom, corroding on her urine mat, lying in a debris of waltzing clerics and medicines. She was a whole person.

'Can you read what it says on the bottles?' Ghazala asked me another time.

I had jammed a finger in a dusty bottle and tried to pull fairy lights from its narrow mouth.

'Can you read English, Noorie?'

'Of course I can,' I said with an air of conceit. 'Johnnie Walker Black Label.'

'Wah wah!' She seemed impressed. 'Madam Noorie. Our Lahori English Madam Noorie.'

When I pulled out the string of fairy lights, they looked dead and depressed in my hand.

'Does Feroze know you're an educated girl?' Ghazala teased.

She had caught us giggling and chitchatting on the terrace several times when he visited Bilquees. I always made sure to serve him a cool glass of Rooh Afza. I had also begun assisting him with the IV and blood pressure machine. I told him that I would someday become a professional nurse.

In return, he brought me gifts. One day it was ripened jamun in a newspaper from a hawker, and on another it was ice cream from McDonald's.

'Hello, Miss Noorie,' he said in English every time he visited. 'How do you do?'

'Fine. Thank you,' I replied.

I pretended not to hear Ghazala's taunt and resumed my duty of emptying bottles.

⁂

Once I'd emptied all the bottles, Bilquees Begum's instructions grew more unusual.

She prayed on a bowl of water and asked me to flick it around the house with my fingers, beckoning the ghost, just as she beckoned me when Muhammad Rauf was not around. 'This is from your Bilquees. I know you're here. I know you've always been here. Come talk to me. Listen to me.' She asked me to say this to the walls, plants, rooms and bottles. I didn't do as I was told for the first few nights. Instead I deceived the dying woman. I roamed aimlessly around the house, from one bottle to the other, saying nothing, and then returned to Bilquees's bedroom after sufficient time had passed, telling her I'd called the ghost but he didn't listen.

'When you see a ghost in one of the bottles,' she commanded, 'you bring it to me.'

'What will it look like?'

'Like a ghost in a bottle.'

After a few nights, I gave in and decided I owed it to Bilquees Begum to try it her way. Around and around the house I went as everyone slept, reciting Bilquees Begum's whimsical lines. Repeating them in hushed corridors. Echoing in green bottles. Whispering them into flower pots on the terrace.

'This is from your Bilquees. I know you're here. I know you've always been here. Come talk to me. Listen to me. I'm dying.'

⁂

I'd been working for Bilquees Begum for almost two months, and a part of me did not want her to die.

I'd begun to enjoy her company, as whenever she was able, she would talk to me about her life and mine. My mother never did that. She never had time. Even before she had a feeble husband to fret over, she had four hungry children to feed.

I started taking more care of Bilquees Begum's appearance. I bathed her, oiled her body and dressed her up in her best clothes. Combed her hair. Parted it here and there. Sometimes I would put a pearl hairpin or a glittery hair band on her head, small treasures that her little granddaughter had left behind. One day, I found an old pair of round sunglasses and a straw hat in one of her bedside drawers. I put them on her and rolled her around the house and the terrace for some air.

We passed an electrician working outside and he snickered at the sickly woman all dolled up.

'Tell Bilquees Begum what you're doing in the house,' I demanded in my most severe voice.

He was standing near the switchboard of the donkey pump with a screwdriver and wire pliers in his hands.

'Sir said there was a short circuit.' He was referring to Muhammad Rauf.

'Look at her and tell her,' I instructed. 'She's the woman of the house. It's her house.'

The electrician looked at Bilquees Begum, who sat stoically in her sunglasses and straw hat, and nervously explained the switchboard repair and the issue with the water motor.

After he finished, Bilquees Begum gently squeezed my hand. I leaned in and pretended that she had whispered something important in my ear.

'Okay, okay. I'll tell him that,' I said. 'Do it fast! Do it properly or she'll get a new electrician.'

'Yes, madam,' he nodded at Bilquees.

I counted all of Bilquees Begum's suits, sweaters, shoes, bedsheets and kitchen appliances. So that nothing else would be stolen. I kept a list, written on paper, with me at all times. 'Remember that red Kashmiri shawl of yours, the one I could not find?' She nodded as if she understood. 'I finally found it beneath a pile of clothes.'

'Shahbash.' She appreciated me and smiled.

With time, I told Bilquees Begum that Feroze and I were becoming close. He and I would sit and talk on the sofa in Bilquees's room or amble on the terrace while she sat in her wheelchair, looking at flowers and plants.

One afternoon, Feroze plucked a small pink Rangoon flower from the creeper and placed it in my palm. He tucked a stray strand of hair behind my ear like they did in Bollywood movies.

'Noorie means light,' he said. 'How can someone whose name means light stay in the shadows, up in that dark room, and have such a depressing life of cleaning other people's shit?'

Shit?

I was hurt when he used that word, when he painted things in my life as they were: drab and dark. Smelly and bleak.

'I want to marry you,' Feroze declared. 'You don't have to do these jobs. I'll talk to my mother. She wanted a fair, beautiful Muslim bride for me, but I don't care about such things. You're beautiful, Noorie. You're beautiful to me.'

I just heard two words, 'marry' and 'you.' Nothing else that came from his lips mattered. No man had ever said that to me before. No man had looked at me in that tender, kind way. I had never had someone listen to me, pay attention to the words that hung from my lips. I had never had someone touch my hand and squeeze my palm as if in fear of losing me. Me? Someone so plain? This kind of warm attention was normally reserved for others. The attention I received from men had always been menacing and foul. I had been groped at a bus station once when I was returning home from my classes. I had kicked the man in his knee and run down the road, petrified. I had been catcalled and flirted with on rickshaw rides. Street corners filled with leering men.

Before I said yes to Feroze's proposal, he cut in. 'Don't say anything. Wait a little, let me speak to my mother first.'

Flushed with excitement, I told Bilquees Begum everything that same night. She said she had loved a man once. A man who was not Muhammad Rauf.

'I know what love is, Noorie. I've seen it,' she said. 'I know what love is. This is not it. This is shit.'

⁂

Bilquees told me her story. We were sitting outside watching black clouds form in the skies. Monsoon season was finally approaching.

She said she had been the beautiful sister growing up. Tall, well groomed, with long brown hair. Her younger sister, Yasmin, had always envied Bilquees's beauty.

Their family belonged to the Jatt caste and had sufficient lands in the village, along with sufficient wealth. When Bilquees and Yasmin grew older, their father and two older brothers sent them to Lahore to receive their BAs. It was at a college function in Lahore that Bilquees first met Waqar Ahmed.

'Isn't it funny that it was at the Christmas play?' Bilquees mused.

Waqar Ahmed was a master's student in their college. He was studying English literature and wanted to take a lectureship in Lahore. His family belonged to a lower-middle-class caste and he was the only child in the family to receive a higher degree.

'There were two good things at that Christmas play,' Bilquees said. 'It was a crammed hall, which meant Waqar and I had to sit next to each other on the steps near the door. And Yasmin was in her room at the hostel, sick with the flu.'

'What did your Waqar look like?' I asked.

'He was a beautiful man,' she said. 'A man who recited Shelley and Ghalib to me in Shalimar Gardens. I could sit in his company for hours and just read or listen to ghazals on my radio. Ghulam Ali and Malika Pukhraj.'

I asked her who Shelley was.

'Percy Bysshe Shelley,' she responded. 'A poet.' Everything should have been fine, according to Bilquees.

She and Waqar had a plan for after graduation. Waqar was to send Bilquees's family an arranged proposal through her neighbour, Gullu auntie.

It was to be a love marriage concealed as arranged.

'You see, you couldn't introduce a man who was not a Jatt to your conservative father and brothers,' said Bilquees. 'It was a different time. It was a difficult time, Noorie. No one in my family married for love, and worse, no one married a non-Jatt.'

One night, Yasmin found one of Waqar's love letters stashed underneath Bilquees's mattress. Bilquees begged her sister not to tell their father and brothers, and for a few months Yasmin held on to the secret.

'I felt a wave of warm affection towards my younger sister.' Bilquees signaled to me to roll her wheelchair inside. Dark, heavy clouds were moving fast above our heads. A drop of rain fell on my face. The sound of evening prayer rang from the nearby mosque.

'People seldom change, Noorie,' she said, out of breath as we moved indoors. Talking was tiring for her. 'They just get better at hiding who they really are.'

I sat on the carpet and watched her perform the evening prayer, which she had to do from her bed. She couldn't stand up. There were dark crescents hanging under her eyes, wrinkles near her mouth and forehead, and blue veins running across her tired limbs.

I tried to picture her as a young woman, a young woman in love. A young woman with dewy soft skin and hair and beauty, but no matter how much I tried, I couldn't imagine her as anything but the frail old woman in front of me.

'When I die,' she said after she finished praying, 'make sure Yasmin doesn't see my body.'

I didn't say anything.

'This is all because of her. This is all because of Yasmin,' she said. 'She never leaves me. She has a hunger for my misery. Make sure her eyes never land on my corpse.'

⁂

For the next week, Bilquees Begum did not speak of Waqar Ahmed or Yasmin. It was as if she had forgotten that she had started to tell me a story, yet every night before I retreated to the rooftop, to the darkness, she still remembered to ask if I had caught the ghost.

Her faith in me was pure, childlike. She was certain I would catch it and bring it to her.

Over the days her pleas to the ghost became more desperate.

'I know you're here. I feel you tower over me when I sleep.'

'Forgive me. This is your Bilquees. I want to see you. Please.'

I had borrowed Bilquees Begum's madness and whimsy. I had even begun to feel a lurking presence myself, especially when I was alone in my room. I placed an empty bottle there too, just in case.

I overheard Mufti Nawaz tell Muhammad Rauf that when people are on their deathbed, ready to descend into a grave, they begin seeing the supernatural and the surreal. They see angels and ghosts, spirit children and demons.

I asked Feroze and Ghazala once if they believed in ghosts, and if they had ever seen one. Feroze said once, at a railway station, he had seen the shape of an old man with a long white beard who vanished suddenly, impossibly. Ghazala scoffed in my face and said I was crazy and that anyone who saw ghosts was crazy too.

One day, I noticed something in one of the bottles in the living room. I hadn't seen it at first. It shuddered slightly on a wooden table, making a soft clinking noise that caught my attention. I jumped up from the kitchen chair and lunged towards it, believing for a moment that I had finally caught the spirit. But there was no ghost, just a moth, trapped inside, fluttering as it tried to escape.

'What are you doing?' Muhammad Rauf's booming voice startled me. The bottle fell from my hands and broke near my feet.

'Stupid girl,' he said. 'Look what you did. You are not meant to touch the decorations. Your tasks are defined.'

I looked at the floor.

'And I see you goofing around with that boy. Stay away or I'll send you back to Sialkot and tell your mother all the impure things you do. Befriending men and whatnot.'

I made a face at him as he turned his back. I did not like him or the big mufti. They had both asked me not to cook or use the same plates that the family used. My Christian hands and mouth had a separate plastic set of plates and cutlery.

The moth did not fly away. It writhed near my foot. I squished it under my chappals.

⌘

Muhammad Rauf went on a week-long religious Tabligh trip with Mufti Nawaz and other clerics. With them gone, I felt freer around the house. Feroze stayed for hours after treating Bilquees Begum. We even snuck out once or twice to parks to spend time with each other.

'Bilquees Begum doesn't think you love me,' I told him as we were sitting in the park, eating ice cream cones.

'What does she know about young people and love?' he mocked. 'She's from a different era. Families married children within families, castes, sects and religions. What does an old woman like her know of love?'

'I don't think she's that old,' I said meekly. 'She's just very sick. Sickness does that.'

My father had shrunk too.

'Whatever it is, don't believe her when she says I do not love you,' he said as he licked his melting ice cream.

'Did you speak to your mother about us? Did you tell her you proposed?' I dropped my head as I asked, afraid of what he might say, and began plucking dry blades of grass with my free hand.

'I will, I will,' he assured me. 'I have to catch Ammi in the right mood. She is very stern on the outside. Inside, she is soft as a melting candle's wax.'

I looked up at him with a steady gaze. He told me to stop playing with the grass and finish my ice cream. It was dripping on my hand.

'You see, my brother married a gori when he was working in Dubai,' he said. 'My mother was upset for a bit but then she gave him permission.'

'A white girl? Really?'

He nodded his head proudly. 'Hmm,' I said.

'You won't have to do these shameful jobs for long. I'll speak to Ammi soon.'

I didn't like the word he used. Shameful. But I remained silent and shyly nodded along.

Bilquees Begum, too, relished her time away from Muhammad Rauf. We played old ghazals on her cell phone. Ustad Amanat Ali Khan. The sitar strumming in the background, the haunting harmonium, the gentle tabla beats like raindrops tapping softly on a windowpane, and his voice, a deep river of sorrow slipping under Bilquees Begum's skin, tugging at the threads of memory and longing. Her sense of sound and smell were weakening, but she could still hear the music clearly if I sat cross-legged on the bed and held the cell phone near her ear.

After a while, she continued telling me her story. Bilquees said that her love affair with Waqar Ahmed continued for a year. He finished his master's and got offered a teaching position in the same college. They celebrated with Yasmin at a restaurant in Mall Road.

All through the dinner, Bilquees could witness Yasmin's fascination with Waqar.

'You see, anyone would fall in love with that man,' Bilquees said. 'His dress shirts and pants, and that nice clean haircut. The way he spoke English, Urdu and Farsi. The way he understood art, history and culture.'

'And he chose no one else but you,' I said.

'And he chose me.'

Like Feroze has chosen me.

When the sisters returned to their village in Narowal after graduating, the family immediately began looking for suitors. Bilquees was every man's first choice, and she was worried that her father and brothers would arrange a match for her with a good Jatt boy because Gullu auntie, the matchmaker, refused to take Waqar's proposal to the Jatt residence.

There were vast acres of land registered under Bilquees and Yasmin's name. Their father wanted them to remain within the family, or at least the caste. He didn't want a boy from the Arain caste to whisk his daughter away. Especially an unsuitable man like Waqar Ahmed, an overlearned man who didn't want the duty of familial lands and crops.

Soon, Bilquees's family settled her engagement with a second cousin. Despite Bilquees's complaints, her family insisted she marry the man. They claimed to know what was better for her.

'Not much is needed in a woman to be called dangerous or difficult in this country,' said Bilquees Begum. 'Just have a mind of your own. Just know who you are and what you want. Families, neighbours and people get terrified easily.'

Bilquees believed that it was after her wedding was decided and planned that Yasmin started eyeing Waqar Ahmed seriously. She had grown fond of him. Although Bilquees kept things to herself, Yasmin would frequently slip Waqar Ahmed's name into their private conversations. She would ask Bilquees how he was, where he was, how he felt about her wedding, and if he had moved on with his life. Yasmin was never good at hiding things.

One day, their mother found a love letter in Yasmin's cupboard. It was addressed to Waqar Ahmed, and in it Yasmin confessed her love and willingness to marry him after Bilquees was settled and shipped off.

'All hell broke loose,' said Bilquees. Their mother held Yasmin by her hair, slapped her across the face, and demanded to know who the boy was. Their mother said that it was the family's mistake to send the girls away from home to a hostel in Lahore. Yasmin blurted out everything. She told everyone about Bilquees and Waqar's romance in Lahore, shifting the blame from sister to sister.

'I became the older sister who had set a bad example for her little sister,' said Bilquees in a faint voice.

The family kept Bilquees and Yasmin locked in the house and said nothing more about the letter and Bilquees's shame—they did not want anyone in the extended family or the neighbourhood to catch wind of their daughter and her former lover. Bilquees's brothers warned her. 'Not a single word about Lahore and that boy. Forget it all.' But Bilquees could not.

After a week or two, the sisters were allowed to do small, safe tasks like visiting the tailor two alleys away, attending an evening tea at a neighbour's house, or sitting through a milad function in a relative's living room. In between these trips, in the quiet moments when people paid her no attention, Bilquees would sneak to the house of a friend, one who knew about the separated lovers and vowed to never betray them, and dial Waqar Ahmed. He promised they would run away together. To Lahore or Karachi, or to his cousin in Birmingham. He did not know for sure. But away from the house full of marigolds and henna. Away from a wedding she did not want.

'Did he come to take you away?' I asked. 'Did he keep his promise?'

'He did,' she said feebly. 'But something happened before I could meet him. Something for which I can never forgive Yasmin.'

⁂

When Muhammad Rauf returned home, he saw several changes in his wife. She had become weaker. Her body had shrivelled, and words disappeared before she could finish a sentence. She was forgetting her prayers. She could not eat or drink. Her eyes were filled with a dreadful weariness. Her body itched and jolted all night long. Her interest in taking care of the house and looking for the ghost also lessened, but in other ways she began relying on me more. She made me sleep on the carpet in her bedroom every night. I was happy to leave my hot room on the roof, even for a hard floor.

Rooms could be violent. The room on the roof, I believed, was very violent. It confronted me. It whispered to me all night. When darkness slipped in and I was up there by myself, the questions slipped in too. *Did I do enough for my family? Will my father ever walk again? Will my mother always have to clean mould and shit? Am I doing enough for Bilquees? Will Feroze ever speak to his mother about me? Is Waqar Ahmed really haunting the hallways? Is he really watching his old lover stretched out before carpenters and electricians, servants and the clerics, dangling between life and death? Is he enjoying her misery? Can we ever forgive other people?*

One night after Bilquees had dozed off, I wandered around the house. I was unable to sleep. I kept thinking about Waqar Ahmed.

I stood on the terrace and looked up at the stormy skies.

It was about to rain.

'Oye Noorie!' I heard someone call my name.

It was Feroze, sitting on his motorbike by the main gate, waving up at me and calling me downstairs.

I tiptoed down the stairs and opened the gate to see him. His hair and white T-shirt were drenched, clinging to his body.

'It's strange it isn't raining in this area of Lahore,' he said. 'It's as if you live in some alternate universe, but don't worry, it'll rain here soon. I've brought cooler weather in this horrid heat.'

I asked him why he was here. What was he doing in the streets so late?

'I told the hospital Bilquees Begum needed me and left,' he winked at me. 'They give us money for food and fuel. Your begum doesn't need me anymore. Even if God comes down now, He cannot save her.'

I did not like that he used her name for free food and money. I didn't have the strength to voice my thoughts out loud, but instead replied, 'You don't know what God is capable of.'

He shrugged off my words as if they did not matter. 'Anyway, I came here to tell you something,' he said calmly. 'I spoke to my mother about you.'

'You did?' My eyes lit up. I moved closer and placed a hand on the motorcycle handlebar.

'She didn't agree. She says she won't let me marry a Christian girl.' His face was serious, and there was no sentiment in his voice, just as there was no sentiment in Muhammad Rauf's voice when he first told me about his dying wife.

'You should go back to Sialkot, Noorie,' he said. 'You'll find someone better.'

My body stiffened. From sadness or anger or both, I did not know. There was a tumult in my heart. I moved away from him slowly. 'You said your brother married a white girl. Didn't your mother have an issue with that?'

'Yes, but she took him with her to America,' he said. 'What would us marrying do for me? I mean … people will mock … my mother would make things difficult …'

My jaw tightened. I looked at him sadly for some time. 'Recite Ghalib.'

'What?'

'Recite Bulleh Shah. Sing me a song. Recite Shelley.'

'I don't know what that is.'

Without a word, I slammed the gate shut and walked back upstairs.

Bilquees was right. This is not love.

As I peered down from the terrace, he was still standing there, looking up at me.

My mind traveled far away. To the village in Narowal, to the cold month of February 1985, to the week of Bilquees's arranged wedding. I remembered the rest of Bilquees's story. Bilquees had waited for everyone in the house to fall asleep.

She had packed her bag to run away with Waqar Ahmed, who was seated on a train heading to her village. They were going to meet in a mustard seed field near her house.

Yasmin had caught Bilquees stuffing her clothes and jewellery in a duffel bag. Yasmin tugged at her sister's arm, begging her not to leave. Not to bring shame on the family. There were relatives coming from out of town.

'I'll make a new life with him,' Bilquees had said to Yasmin.

'They'll marry me off to some strange man as a punishment for your sins,' Yasmin sobbed.

Bilquees did not reply. She kept stuffing things inside the bag. Aghast, Yasmin took a few steps back and ran out of the room.

Bilquees quickly zipped the bag with her trembling hands. She had barely crossed her courtyard when her father yanked her back by her hair. The family locked her in her bedroom and barred the windows. Yasmin had betrayed her once more.

'It was such a blurry, hazy night,' Bilquees narrated. 'I remember howling and shrieking. I remember my brother hitting me across my face, shouting words at me. I remember tasting blood. I remember being locked in that bedroom full of henna and bangles, pounding at the door. And after a few hours, I remember hearing a gunshot coming from outside the house.'

When Bilquees heard the gunshot, she dropped to her knees in defeat, the vibrations echoing in her ears. She curled into a fetal position, surrendering before her family and God. She knew instantly what had happened. She knew her lover was waiting for her in the mustard seed fields. She knew her family would not allow that.

Bilquees got married. Her brother spent only a night in jail. Their father used family contacts and paid off the judge, who waived everything in the name of self-defense. He said Waqar Ahmed had been stalking and harassing Bilquees.

Waqar Ahmed's family did not have any money, nor did they have the power to contact lawyers and appeal for a trial. His family collected his body from the morgue. The soil in the mustard seed absorbed his blood, and Bilquees Begum did not say his name for thirty-two years.

'I've paid my price,' she said. 'The more I ran away from the past, and his name, the more it haunted me. I've seen him in rivers, bridges, flower pots and bottles. Now, I have nothing to do but rot in this bed and think about my Waqar.'

I trembled as my mind painted a picture. Waqar Ahmed lying dead in a sea of yellow and green. Specks of his blood on a blooming mustard flower.

Feroze blew a whistle to get my attention again. I stared down at him from my spot on the terrace. He was folding his hands over his head, asking for forgiveness. I picked up a small tinted glass bottle next to a potted plant and threw it from the rooftop near his motorbike.

He jumped back from the shattered glass, yelled to the skies that I was crazy, and sped away from Bilquees Begum's house. I returned to the barsati to lie down on my bed and weep, alone.

⁂

The next morning, Ghazala stood near my charpoy on the rooftop, shaking me awake. She said Bilquees Begum was asking for me. She was not feeling well.

I heard the thudding of Ghazala's feet as she descended the stairs. I sank my feet into my chappals and stood up, preparing to join her in Bilquees's room. Out of the corner of my eye, a flicker caught my attention, When I turned, I saw light yellow smoke swirling, frothing out of the bottle I had placed by my bed. Stumbling, I picked up the bottle and stared inside. I thought I saw a face—a thin jaw, dark eyes and a small mouth in the smoke.

I ran downstairs to Bilquees Begum with the bottle. Muhammad Rauf was standing by his wife's bed, holding her hand. As she saw me enter the room, she let go of his hand and reached for me.

'What is this?' asked Muhammad Rauf as I showed the bottle to Bilquees.

I ignored him and turned to her. 'You're right. He's here. He's been haunting you, watching over you for years.'

'What is this stupidity?' Muhammad Rauf was confounded.

Bilquees Begum gave me a blank stare. Her fingers touched the glass, and then they dropped. It was as if she did not remember anything. Not the stories, not Waqar, not the mustard seed fields. That young girl had evaporated overnight, leaving behind an empty, decaying carcass.

Her mouth released a low gurgle. She shivered and closed her eyes.

Bilquees Begum passed away that morning holding my hand.

⁂

It poured heavily on the day of the funeral. It felt like the house itself would drown; it was full of dirty teacups, water pitchers, guests and the sweet smell of the jasmine attar. I was not allowed to bathe Bilquees Begum for the last rites; instead I could only look at her and clean up afterwards.

Mufti Nawaz's wife and Bilquees Begum's eldest daughter washed the body. They cut off Bilquees Begum's kameez, removed her diaper, and put cotton rolls in her nose and ears. They dressed her in a plain white shroud and flicked rose water with their fingers.

And then, she was ready to be submitted to the dirt, to God, to the things that had been promised.

I scrubbed the floors after everyone left. I swept away the rose petals, neem leaves and dirt from people's shoes. I threw away the diaper and the clothes in which she died. I washed the glass from which she last drank. I cleaned and packed the wheelchair so Muhammad Rauf could donate it to a hospital. I kept on a shelf the glass bottle in which I had seen smoke and ghost. When I had gone to collect it from her room after she died, it was empty and cold. No trace of the smoke.

⁂

The next day, a new party of mourners arrived. They had arrived from Karachi on a train to pay condolences to Muhammad Rauf. The travel took a day and a half.

The oldest woman in the family was in her sixties. She was blind from a cataract surgery gone wrong years earlier. She wore a pair of black sunglasses and held a bamboo cane in her hand.

I held her gently by her arm and guided her to the bathroom when she wanted to perform ablution for Isha prayer at night. I stood by the door holding her cane and sunglasses and watched her clean her feet with a Muslim shower. I looked at her reflection in the mirror. Her eyes were steel grey.

'How do you know Bilquees Begum?' I asked with curiosity.

'I'm her younger sister,' the woman said. 'Yasmin.'

I frowned but was relieved that the frail, blind guest could not see the disdain in my eyes. She moved her hands around trying to locate my shoulder or arm so I could direct her outside the bathroom. Her right hand slammed on the wooden door and she whimpered from pain. I reached for her quickly.

'Come,' I said calmly as I put my arms around her shoulder. She held my hand and thanked me. Her hands, her fingers looked exactly like my Bilquees Begum's. My rancour melted into pity and sadness.

'Let me take you outside,' I said as she prayed loudly to God for my happiness.

I lay upside down on a charpoy on the terrace, looking around at Bilquees's flower pots and creepers, her clothes drying on the clothesline, the line of bottles she had collected, the flaking white walls; I looked at all the things she had left behind. All the years she had spent on that house. Distracting herself.

Time did not stop. The house did not crumble once the woman of the house died. Nothing really happened.

Ghazala kept doing laundry and dishes. Muhammad Rauf went to work and prayed. The world kept moving. Life, unyielding, carried on.

But I believed the house needed to mourn, too. After the guests had departed and the residents had retreated into slumber, the house needed to wail as well.

If I looked at all the relationships, all the tangled lines I had seen in that house over the months I was there, if I looked at everything on the surface, there was abundant love everywhere.

Muhammad Rauf had loved Bilquees. Bilquees must have loved her husband at some point, and she definitely loved Waqar. Ghazala loved the house and her duty. Feroze loved me, or at least I had thought he did. And I loved Feroze. But if I looked very closely, if I lay upside down on a charpoy or stood quietly enveloped in darkness and shadows and looked again, there was no love anywhere. No one loved anyone. No one loved anything. It was all smoke, vanishing in a small bottle. It was all an illusion.

'Get up, girl.' Muhammad Rauf's voice roused me from my thoughts. He was standing before me. Imposing. Daunting. Like a demon.

I stood up from the charpoy and fixed my dupatta.

'You can go back home now,' he said, handing me my salary. 'You're no longer needed.'

I counted the wrinkled notes shamelessly in front of him, and then protested that I needed three thousand rupees more.

'And why is that?'

I lied and told him Bilquees had promised me a raise for doing such a good job.

'Your kind is never loyal, is it?' he sneered as he handed me another two thousand rupees.

'No, sir,' I said, looking straight into his eyes. 'And when you yourself are dying, make sure to get a Muslim caregiver.' He mumbled something and told me to pack my belongings and leave first thing in the morning.

When he left, I shoved my clothes and money in a bag. As I was zipping it, I noticed a small piece of paper sticking out from underneath a dupatta.

I remembered the fortune-teller and the parrot from the bus station when I first arrived. I took out the scrap and read my fortune again, after months. *Dive into the darkness and let it consume you. In the end, you'll see clearly, the truth revealed in the shadows.*

⁂

Eight months had passed since I'd left Bilquees's house.

I returned home, worked in a textile factory for six months, saved some money and then continued with college. I did not stay in Sialkot. I moved back to Lahore after a college offered me a Christian Fellowship scholarship. My father died three days after I started classes.

Our family, after a long mourning period, eventually turned to healing. Mother collapsed one night in my arms as

I lay on the rooftop, counting the stars, and began to cry. I let her. I just held her and let her.

Mother saved to repaint our house to make it look less dismal. Between moving the furniture, scouring the floors with detergent, sweeping every nook and cranny, and rearranging the room for a new beginning, we found a stack of money taped underneath a table. There was an Urdu note in my father's handwriting.

For Noorie's college. For little ones' school. For my wife.

He must have forgotten about the money after the stroke caught him. Mother and I looked at each other, silently. What could have been said in that moment?

'What a good man,' is all she said, wiping away a tear.

⌘

When I spotted Ghazala again, it was at a vegetable market in Lahore. She was bickering with a vendor over the rising prices of potatoes and onions.

'Arey Lahori English Madam Noorie!' she exclaimed when I poked her shoulder.

Her ten-year-old son stood beside her, eating roasted corn and watching a video on his cell phone.

'It's been so long,' said Ghazala. 'It's March now. Can you imagine?'

She told me that three weeks after the funeral, Muhammad Rauf went to Chitral and married a seventeen-year-old girl. Her father had just died, and her uncle sold her to Muhammad Rauf. He said he was doing a service to God. It was all for Allah's reward, to give shelter to a poor orphan.

Muhammad Rauf made Ghazala sell all of the empty bottles to a scrap dealer. The new bride did not find such decor amusing. Many of Bilquees's clothes, shawls and bedsheets went missing after the funeral days, when Muhammad Rauf was in Chitral.

Mufti Nawaz had opened a beauty salon and boutique in Karachi and London. And Feroze married his cousin and invited Muhammad Rauf and his bride to the ceremony. Ghazala had never seen so much glitter on a wedding card before.

All the time that she chatted, I kept looking at her yellow kameez. I had seen it somewhere, but I could not figure out where exactly. Then, suddenly, I remembered.

'I don't recall Bilquees Begum giving you this shirt,' I said. 'And that wallet you have. I think I saw that in her cupboard!'

I expected her to deny it. I expected her to feel shame. But she was brazen. Proud, almost.

'And what was she to do with all of her clothes, appliances, and all?' Ghazala snickered. 'Take it to her grave?'

When she left after hailing a rickshaw, I watched the kameez flutter in the wind as the green vehicle zoomed away.

It had been one of Bilquees Begum's favourite shirts. Bright yellow with green embroidered flowers.

The colours of the mustard plant.

My Bones Hold a Stillness

The memorial for the dead exchange student was to take place in the town mosque on the Fourth of July.

I wanted to stay inside the apartment, curled up in bed with a book. Peeling back the thick comforter, stripping off my pajamas, and taking a shower seemed like a daunting task.

Franny, my roommate, kept pestering me. She insisted we go to the grocery store and then to the memorial in the evening. I had been relying on milk, cereal and Knorr's cheddar broccoli rice-pasta blend for days.

I believed there was no point in attending the memorial. The girl was dead. It had already been six weeks. The white boy who shot her in the narrow high school hallway had been taken into custody and declared insane by several leading newspapers, in articles that often referred to him as a 'loner' and referenced some vague 'mental illness'. Every paper featured his picture on the front page. He grinned widely while in police custody.

His teeth were ugly. His hair was ugly. The orange prison jumpsuit was ugly. Everything about him was ugly.

No newspaper spoke enough of the ugliness.

At the grocery store, Franny and I juggled frozen rice and pasta and regretted not getting a cart, as I ranted about how no newspaper was discussing the sixteen-year-old Pakistani student he had killed. Franny swiveled her head towards me and asked me not to speak so loudly. Told me that I was making the people in the store uncomfortable.

So I pursed my lips and kept quiet. I silenced myself, made myself uncomfortable, so that the people around me would not feel uncomfortable, too.

⁂

University was closed for the summer. The university library functioned on limited hours, and in those limited hours, I sat in uncomfortable wooden chairs with lukewarm coffee and worked diligently on my undergraduate English thesis. The only other place besides the grocery store and the library that I was willing to go was the small pond near a farm owned by a classmate's uncle, a man named Mr Oat. I liked dipping my feet in the water and sitting next to Franny in silence. I liked to look at the trees—hickory, sycamore and basswood—how everything was in place, perfectly arranged: the leaves, twigs, trunk, roots.

Nothing in nature fell apart.

The exchange student's foster family and her real family back home started a GoFundMe after her death. Many people in town chipped in for funeral arrangements, for the kafan, and the cost of shipping her body back to Pakistan in a cargo plane. She arrived here, in America, as a scholar, and yet she did not have the chance to walk through customs with her degree and convocation cap. She returned home to Islamabad, embalmed, in a foreign body bag.

I did not realize that I *also* kept calling her 'the girl', 'the dead girl', and 'the scholarship girl' until Franny told me to be more sensitive and say her name.

'She was from *your* country,' Franny said. 'She came here on a scholarship like you. She was running away from things in her past like you. Say her name. She was a person.' I tried, but my lips would not release her name. I could think it, turn the letters over in my mind and repeat her name to myself, silently, over and over again. But when I opened my mouth to speak, I found that the name would not come. 'You're doing the same thing the newspapers are doing,'

Franny continued. 'Don't complain about them, then.'

I had seen the girl, Dur-e-Shahwar, several times around the small town and on campus. The first time was at a meeting for the International Student Association. She was in high school and I was in university, but sometimes the two schools held events together and shared clubs for the more isolated student groups. The groups not big enough to merit their own clubs at their own schools. There were only a handful of us at the International Student Association event, and though we came from all across the world, from the outside our stories and needs must have looked the same. Dur-e-Shahwar and I spotted each other from across the room and nodded politely in recognition. After that, I saw her everywhere. In the town library, at the pharmacy, crossing the street downtown, at the post office. We never spoke, merely smiled at each other as we passed by.

I could tell that there had been times when she wanted to talk to me. Sometimes at the grocery store or at other places, I would catch her shifting body from the corner of my eye. It was a careful dance. She would take a step or two in my direction and then, to my relief, she would have a change of heart and vanish behind a wall, through a door, or down a different aisle.

Dur-e-Shahwar was young enough and lonely enough to seek me out, to try to make me her surrogate, out-of-country older sister.

But I did not want to be anyone's anything at that time.

Around the time Dur-e-Shahwar first arrived at the high school, I had just been struck by the news of my mother's death back home. I felt like I could not breathe, like someone had trapped me in a bell jar, the air inside swiftly depleting. There were nights I crawled inside my closet in a stupor, lay in the fetal position, and wept. For how long, I could not say. I did not remember. I was happy Dur-e-Shahwar and I never spoke during the five months before she was shot. If we had, her dying would have cut at the vulnerable parts of myself, stirred too many emotions, and untied countless knots inside me.

It would have opened up the abyss. And saying Dur-e-Shahwar's name aloud, I felt, made her more real. More alive—wandering around town by herself, deciphering menus at coffee shops. Flat White. Maple Latte. Pumpkin Spice. All by herself. To speak her name would be to acknowledge that she was a person, a person who hoped and dreamed and laughed and died. To speak her name would be to kill her, to make her dead. More dead. The real person no longer here, everything alive about her now gone forever.

⌘

Dur-e-Shahwar Fatima's funeral was held in a baseball field four days after the shooting. I did not attend but heard about it from Bushra, a neighbour in our apartment complex who found me in the laundry room a few days after. Bushra told me that the baseball field was crammed with mourners. Dur-e-Shahwar's casket had been open for a brief period, and from her seat Bushra was able to see the body covered in a white shroud, gifted by a Bengali Muslim family. There was makeup, too, lots of makeup on Dur-e-Shahwar's face, something which was not allowed in Islamic funerals but had to be done to conceal the gunshot wounds.

She had been shot under her ear, in her neck, and on the back of the leg.

'Poor girl,' Bushra said to me as she peeled lavender-scented dryer sheets out of a box. 'She fought against her parents in Gujrat to follow her dreams. She came here to become something ...' Bushra sniffled loudly, wiping tears from her eyes.

I was folding a tank top with the words Positive Vibes Only written across the chest.

Bushra continued to speak over the thumping sounds of the washing machines. She told me that Dur-e-Shahwar had told another girl at the mosque during Friday prayers that there was a white boy in her class who often stared at her in the hallway. They had a few classes together. Maybe he wanted to be her friend? Dur-e-Shahwar did not know what to make of it. She did not know how to make the few friends she *did* have at school understand why this made her so uncomfortable. She felt her American friends would call her conservative, prudish even, about the opposite sex, and her family would have demanded that she return home.

They would have told her that America was unsafe. Dur-e-Shahwar did not want to lose her newfound freedom because of a boy and his strange looks.

This detail was new to me. I felt a tingling sensation at the back of my neck. Fear stirred inside me.

'She loved painting too, you know,' Bushra said. 'She was an artistic kid. Painting. Pottery. Have you seen that wall covered with graffiti under the bridge at the park?'

I nodded without looking at Bushra as I watched my blue towel spin in the washing machine. Franny and I had stumbled upon the graffiti wall together during a long walk, and she had deemed it beautiful. She knew art. She had studied it in school. She often discussed it as one might discuss old lovers—intimately, noting their charms and flaws. She noticed the eerie quiet in Monet's misty gardens, and the madness in Sadequain's brooding figures. So when she said she found the graffiti beautiful, I trusted her opinion.

'Do you know the drawing of the girl with wings?' Bushra asked. 'That was her. She did that.'

I silently took in Bushra's words, thinking of this small act of belonging.

'I spoke to her foster family, who live in South Park,' Bushra continued. 'Her sister told me that back in Gujrat, Dur-e-Shahwar survived poverty, dengue, and then, over here ...'

'She ended up dying in the arms of a classmate who probably couldn't even pronounce her name,' I cut in without batting an eye.

Bushra cast me a horrified look, her face creased with worry. She picked up her bag of clean washing and left me in the laundry room. I knew what she was thinking. That I was shamelessly insensitive. I was used to this. Used to people thinking I was cold and insensitive. I always thought I was just being honest.

My family in Rawalpindi said that about me too. They did not like how I handled Ammi's death. They believed I dealt with it too quietly, and in secret. Mourning was a different kind of celebration back home. Mourning one's parents should be a grand affair. Almost ceremonious. People should witness the wreck, the diving into the abyss, and the toiling out of it. But I did not rush back to Pindi to perform ghusl on Ammi's body or ready her for the burial. I did not prepare the funeral food or cater to the mourners, who had not seen my mother in years but who still wanted to talk about how extraordinary she was.

Instead, I vanished inside a crevice, and then that crevice became a womb, and then a labyrinth, and then I was lost within it. I had imprisoned myself in my bedroom. I stayed there, immobile, chewing on terrible frozen food and drinking soda. Contrary to what everyone believed, my mourning was menacingly grand. But I did not need to share it. It started as a small flame, flickering in the depths of my stomach, until it began to spread and the fire hit me like a lightning bolt. Struck me silent. Left a little ember. A fire started and swallowed me whole, burning every single cell in my body and every strand of hair on my head until

I was nothing but ash. My body became a vessel of flames. The flesh charred. Everything burnt, every single cell in the body burnt, every black strand on the head burnt, the buttons on the coats caught on fire, everything in and on me yowled. Then, the fire leapt out of my body and became a storm. A thunder rumbled through me. A flood cooled down the ferocious fire. Cooled me down. Defused the burning flames. The wavering white smoke fizzled away. And left nothing but ash.

No harness. No bearing.

Lifeless. Lying inside smoke and vapour. For months, I was nothing but ash. An incorporeal thing. Formless. Limited. Waiting for grass, ghost pipes, bluebells and wild mushrooms to grow around me.

Ash.

Guilt wrecks people. It chews them right up. Letting go of it is like crab-walking down a spiral staircase. One step forward. Many steps back. And by the end of it all, you're dizzy and nauseous.

The whole act was useless and tiresome. After six months of struggling through the darkness and numbness, I arranged for Franny to move in as my roommate. She enjoyed psychoanalyzing me, wondering why I was so numb to everything—or had I become numb with time? And why did I not speak aloud about things—sorrowful things, the torrents of my heart, the poems I liked and read over and over again in solitude, the songs I listened to as a child, the week I spent in a psych ward after Ammi's death? Most of all she tried to understand why I did not speak of my life back home. 'I spoke a lot, you know,' I told her one day as we were removing batteries from the smoke detector so we could light our cigarettes inside. 'I fought with my parents, though it didn't do any good.'

Franny responded by telling me that she'd had the unhappiest of childhoods. She never kept in touch with her alcoholic stepfather, who used to hit her, and she was ostracized by those nasty kids who tormented her in middle school for having big breasts. I already knew all that. We talked about it often.

I let Franny heal me, and in that, she healed herself. Hemmed the invisible wounds. I could see traces of sorrow in her eyes on days she became very quiet and went to the apartment balcony to smoke by herself. I didn't know where her memories took her, but I assumed it was a joyless place.

Grief turns people into liars.

My friend was a good liar. And so was I. We lied to each other. And to ourselves. We played a dangerous game. She chose to live as a person without a past. My past glided above me, a noose around my neck.

⌘

My mother's death was not natural or an accident. She did not pass away in her sleep like my grandfather, or my paternal aunt, who, in wild ignorance and a mad fit of frenzy, swallowed blood pressure medication when her blood pressure was already low.

Ammi killed herself.

Abba never told anyone about the sleeping pills except for me. The rest of the family accepted the lie that one morning, Ammi simply did not wake up. What was so hard to fathom? Many things can happen to a sleeping body. Cardiac arrest?

Brain haemorrhage? Sudden arrhythmic death? No one could suspect suicide.

Mothers are supposed to be reservoirs, deep wells of patience, discipline, compromise, self-sacrifice. Mothers waltz into burning rooms and they always, *should* always, resurrect. They are immortal. They live on through the silverware on the kitchen shelves and the shape of your hand.

A mother might kill herself metaphorically, but not literally. A mother might willingly kill her ambition, her past desires, her body for the higher purpose of making and mothering children and mending husbands, but a mother cannot be that irrational, that selfish and chaotic, that she ends it all. Who would take care of her children, her children's children, her husband, the curtains and the dust accumulated on the glass vase in the drawing room?

How could that even make sense? A mother losing her will to pass the hours in a day. A mother taking pills to sleep forever and leave the rest of the world to struggle in her wake.

It happened. Ammi killed herself.

And she killed herself because of me. Because of something I told her years ago. Her heart was heavy. She nursed a secret she could not share. The invisible weight of unshared grief collapsed on her. The body just seized up.

Back in the apartment, Franny and I put the groceries away and got into the car to drive to the memorial.

We sat cross-legged on the blue carpet inside the mosque with the imam, a few Muslim neighbours, and some unfamiliar high school students who still wanted to talk about Dure-Shahwar with everyone in attendance.

The rest of the town carried on with farmers' markets and tailgate parties, the Fourth of July parade and the fireworks preparation. Six weeks was enough to mourn and remember the blood in the school hallways and the toppled tables in the cafeteria. The trial for the white boy with the big grin was pending, and the dead girl was shipped off and buried far away. There was no need to speak further about uncomfortable things. There was no need to talk about the ten-thousand-dollar GoFundMe for the shipment of the coffin. At least for a while.

There were mentions, at the memorial, of how great Dur-e-Shahwar was, what a fun adventure she had been having in America, what she wanted to do in the future, and how sad it was that her life was cut short by a gruesome, violent, senseless act.

The imam recited the Quranic verses of patience, closure, and empathy, of leaving this earth and forgiving. He asked us to offer a prayer for Dur-e-Shahwar so she could find her home in heaven.

I leaned over to Franny and whispered, 'That bastard. He doesn't know the damage he's caused.'

'Which bastard?' She looked puzzled.

I bit my lip and stayed quiet until Franny nudged me. 'The boy with the gun,' I said. 'The reason we're here with our heads bowed. He's no idea what he's done. He's taken away chances and opportunities from so many petrified young women back home. Do you think their families will allow them to leave Pakistan now? To leave a place that chokes them, only to go to a place that shoots them?'

Franny pouted and looked straight ahead at the imam, who was now inviting a girl from Dur-e-Shahwar's class to the podium to say a few words.

'Rather than freeing them ...' I kept mumbling, and Franny kept listening, though whether to me or to the imam, I wasn't sure.

I didn't know how to explain why I was so angry, so sad, but sitting in the mosque, I knew I wanted something more. Something grand. I wanted protests, rebellions. Loud chants pillorying the white shooter. I wanted everyone to promise me that school corridors would be safe, grocery stores would be safe. I wanted everyone to remember Dur-e-Shahwar—the exchange student from Gujrat who was shot next to her high school locker. Dur-e-Shahwar—who was probably dutifully reciting the prayers, Darood Sharif and Ayatul Kursi in her heart for protection as she bled out on a classmate's lab coat. I wanted to be able to say her name.

'There will be no justice, will there?' I asked Franny.

'Don't say that.'

I wanted to remind her of another high school shooting, only a few months prior, where the shooter was sent to rehab and not prison. And another shooting a few months before that where the shooter barely received any news coverage. And who knew if he was acquitted or set free? But perhaps a memorial was not the place to think of fears, grievances and facts. It was a place to listen to the imam's wisdom and the high school student's story of how once Dur-e-Shahwar gave her sandwich to a homeless man.

I tried, but after a while I felt like I could not breathe inside the mosque. I held Franny's hand and completed a breathing exercise I had learned from a meditation app on my phone.

'Everyone has amnesia when it comes to violence,' I whispered.

I was afraid, afraid that the boy, the carnage and Dur-e-Shahwar's name would dissolve behind the noise of fireworks and the smoke from barbecue parties. Everything would fade into the background after a while. The boy's crime would be forgotten and he would continue living in a juvenile detention centre or a mental health facility. That was the extent of the justice Dur-e-Shahwar would get, her family would get.

The boy would continue living, while she was dead. He would carry on.

It did not matter what kind of a life the boy would have—he would still eat and bathe and complain about food while she disintegrated into gas, mould and bones. Decomposed. Ruined.

⁂

We are catacombs of trauma, reservoirs of hurt, and when my uncle touched me for the first time, I was six.

Ammi's cousin was visiting Pakistan for the summer from Florence, where he lived by himself. He coaxed me into the dingy storeroom on the rooftop, full of forgotten scraps from around the house. He said he had brought me a doll from Florence, a doll he described in great detail—porcelain, handmade with rosy cheeks, locks of golden hair and eyes like a blue river. I had just learned to spell the word river in school.

There was no doll up in the storeroom. Just us.

This continued through the lead-up to his marriage that same summer. My cousins applied henna on my little hands for his mehndi ceremony. My mother stitched me a pink frock. My uncle continued to take me to the storeroom on the rooftop until he moved with his new wife back to Italy. They had two sons there. He kept sending my mother letters and photographs. Pictures in which he smiled wide. He posed. He carried on. He lingered in my life even though he was miles away.

When he visited Pindi again, I had just turned eleven. And when he touched me again, he said it was out of love. There was something endearing about me, something that the flowers and the birds in Italy did not give him. He left an invisible imprint on my body.

Through the years, my mind kept the sharp, vivid memories of all the encounters. The dark storeroom. The hot rooftop. They never seemed to release me. They never faded. I was stuck inside those rooms. My bedroom, glowing pink from a lamp near my bed. I remembered other details, too. My jeans. His cigarette breath. His shalwar. My little fingers. My red dupatta in my mouth.

My body turned into a house I no longer owned. I simply paid rent to exist in it. My body became a piece of colonized land. It was no longer something I owned, a homeland. My teenage years were crumbling, immersed in chaos. My legs were laced with cigarette burns I concealed underneath jeans and shalwars. My nights carried me back to the hot room on the rooftop. I barely slept unless I took sleeping pills.

Neighbours and relatives saw me around the city, skipping school, wearing tight jeans and T-shirts and smoking shamelessly in public. They reported to Ammi. The verdict was that I was going astray. Finding a husband could tame me before I turned twenty; they persuaded Ammi and she began her search for a suitable suitor.

When I finally told Ammi about my uncle, it was the winter I turned sixteen. I told her I had not slept in years. My body constantly ached. I washed it several times a day, scoured every part, rinsed it clean to wash away the stains from the dark room, but it still smelled of cigarettes, of him. My parents had wondered why I took so many showers. Why I scrubbed until my neck and arms were pink, why I was so careless, so shameful to waste so much water.

After I told her the truth, Ammi's face was a kaleidoscope of anger, then grief, then denial. She withdrew for a few days, then reemerged, convinced I must have misremembered what had transpired many summers ago. Determined to persuade me that I might have been hallucinating. I had watched too many modern movies. I was out to get my uncle. Why? She did not know, but I was.

It was easier for Ammi to believe that her daughter was a wicked liar than to accept the truth that her own cousin, whom she had honoured and invited into her house, could do something so appalling. How could she recover from this if it were true?

I did what was asked. Stayed quiet for the sake of the family, to keep my good name. I told myself that it had not happened, and I told my body that it had not happened. But the damage stayed coiled inside me like a serpent.

I persuaded myself that pain is just an idea, a fabrication we create, and that if we bury it and blot memories, it becomes quiet, deathly quiet. Eventually it might even slither away. The mind, too, forgives and forgets. But the body collects every wound. Repressed pain loomed over my bed and descended when I fell asleep. Everything reverberated in my stolen body. His touch. The room. Ammi's denial. Everything echoed in my bones.

⌘

Franny and I walked quietly outside the mosque after the service was finished and watched the high school students plant a magnolia tree in the backyard.

In loving memory of Dur-e-Shahwar. May your spirit soar.

'When this magnolia blossoms, I'm sure her spirit will visit,' said a student. 'She will sit on the branches and pluck the white flowers.'

There were nods around the crowd.

It was a sweet wish. But I was certain her spirit would not consider gliding through US customs to return to that town, lurk around that tree and swing from its branches. My patience was ebbing. I wanted to leave. And to Franny's surprise, I did not want to head back to the apartment. I wanted to drive around.

'That's an improvement,' she teased. 'First, that wild display of anger, and now, an adventure. You must be getting better.'

American flags, red, white and blue, fluttered outside gas stations, convenience stores and houses as we drove away in my Subaru. Music roared from frat houses and the backyards of otherwise silent houses. Neighbourhoods were overrun with dog walkers and children on bicycles.

We drove by the high school where Dur-e-Shahwar was shot. I slowed the car so Franny and I could look at the place. Confront it after spending an hour remembering Dur-e-Shahwar. We had stayed away since the shooting.

The stairs outside the school doors were bare. Long gone were the flowers and teddy bears and signs of love and remembrance that had been left after the shooting.

No Firearms Beyond This Point, a sign outside the doors cautioned.

'You know I read somewhere that when the school reopens, the kids won't be allowed to bring their school bags,' Franny said softly as she leaned over from the passenger seat to look at the building. 'And someone who teaches there told me that before the shooting, the principal had discussed revamping their security systems. Too late, though.'

I looked at the red bricks and white windows. 'Sometimes I wonder,' I began, 'if Dur-e-Shahwar had stayed in Gujrat, would she still be alive?'

'Or she could be dead there too,' Franny said. 'Dead in a different kind of way. Who's to say?'

It was then that Franny asked me to tell her why I left home and came to America. The rays from the early evening sun illuminated her brown hair. She looked like a divine spiritual entity.

'If you think about it, no one wants to leave home unless they're very unhappy,' Franny answered herself. 'Or if there's a void that home can't fill.'

Franny might have been right. No one wants to leave the comfort of the sunny courtyard neighbourhood where people saw them grow up, leave their families and gardens only to come to a place where they have to shovel piles of snow every winter, sit alone at cafés with no friends, learn a new language at a lifeless community centre, memorize strange road rules, learn how to file taxes, how to survive on shitty health insurance. No one wants to begin again unless they have to.

Franny told me once that she had tried to run away several times when she was young. She told me that she was caught and brought back home every time. On one occasion, someone called the cops when they saw her waiting for a bus, alone, at midnight. She was nine. Another time, she ran all night through the woods, hoping to lose her way and end up somewhere new. For hours she ran, but when morning arrived, she discovered that all the miles she'd covered had only returned her to her own house. To her stepfather. To her absent mother.

'I don't know,' Franny said. 'Sometimes you can't reason with people at home. Running away, leaving it all behind, is the only thing that makes it easier.'

'Does it?' I asked. 'Does it make it easier?'

'It should. That's what I tell myself.'

'Do you think he targeted her for a reason?' I asked.

'I can't say,' Franny said, her face forlorn. 'He tried to kill other people too. Who knows what he was thinking?'

I looked at the grass, the trees, and the stairs one more time before driving away from the building. In the coming years, students would graduate and teachers would resign and everyone would take with them a piece, a memory, of Dur-e-Shahwar even if they did not know it. What happened in that building would be important. With time, she would become less so.

'He had a name for the gun, you know,' I said as we drove away. 'The Silencer.'

Pain makes a home inside a body.

It is a shape-shifter.

It stays awake in unfamiliar crevices. It sleeps in the folds of your skin. Stays collected in the wrinkles on your face. It is relentless when not dealt with properly, when it is not listened to.

My confession and my mother's denial created a divide between us. She resented me for inventing such a mad story about a member of the family who was so close to God. By fifty, he had become a deeply religious man with a long beard. He made his daughter wear a veil to school.

At eighteen, I was presented before eligible suitors and their mothers in our drawing room with tea trolleys and samosas. The hope was that I would settle down. I was wildly unhappy. That summer, a cousin stayed with us and I told her everything I had told my mother.

We were on the rooftop, forced there due to a power outage in the neighbourhood. She had just finished ninth grade and I was reading Plath's poetry to her under my phone's flashlight. We watched the dark streets and, here and there, a vendor with a lowly yellow bulb hanging on top of his cart. The mangoes, peaches, lychees and watermelon glowed beneath the light.

My uncle was planning a visit to Pakistan, his first in seven years, and my body had started to tremble again. He was planning to move back permanently. He did not want his children to grow up around alcohol and sex.

I started telling the story as we sat in the dark, letting it soar, roam free, and pollute the air between us. I waited for her to shrug it off or walk out, offended by the accusation, to deny it as my mother had done. But instead, she held my hand.

'I'm going to run away,' I said. 'I've applied to a college in the States, and I'm going soon.'

'Not everything can be dealt with by running away,' my cousin said, teary-eyed. 'I heard a character say that in a film.'

'True. Maybe you're right. Maybe trauma carries a passport too. Maybe it doesn't burn in a pyre. It doesn't just disintegrate. Who knows?'

⁂

It was seven in the evening.

Franny and I sat across from each other at a Japanese restaurant. She watched me eat sushi rolls and slurp noodle broth. She wasn't hungry. I was. I was famished.

'Easy now,' she said gently. 'It's like you haven't eaten in a year.'

'I really haven't eaten in a year,' I replied. She nodded.

'You know, when my mother married my stepfather,' Franny said, 'she stopped eating. She became very frail.'

'Do you sometimes wonder why she never left him?' I asked. 'You picked up and left. I did. She did.' We both knew who I was referring to.

'I could never tell, growing up. It felt so easy to blame her. I thought my mother chose to be distraught. To stay in that rotten trailer with that rotten man.'

'Do you think we inflict pain on ourselves on purpose?'

'We might, sometimes. Unknowingly. Or we have no choice but to stay in the darkness,' she replied. 'There must be so many Frannys and Durs lying somewhere in silence because they have to. And sometimes it's easier than we think to hike out of the hole.'

I dug my fork into my last maki roll and played around with it on the plate. A pair of chopsticks lay untouched. I was never taught how to use them, and I had never tried to learn.

'It's awfully quiet inside the abyss,' I confessed. 'Painfully lonely too. God knows I tried to drag people inside so it was less frightening. So they could find me a way out.'

My body shuddered as I remembered the storeroom, Ammi ...

'See, when you're inside the abyss, you call out for help,' I said. 'And I did. I did call out for help. No one believed me. They believed *him*. He carried on. He still carries on. And I'm stuck between returning to a home without my mother and staying in this new place where I can be shot outside a grocery store. I'm afraid to go back and I'm terrified of staying.' Franny folded her arms on the table as she listened quietly.

Her eyes were focused only on my face. The restaurant, the food, the hum of conversation and the clatter of metal on porcelain vanished. Nothing existed. Just us. Just my painful words suspended in the air.

'Look at us,' I joked. 'Discussing morbid things while high school students are out getting drunk under bridges.'

Franny gave a low laugh. 'Okay, Nietzsche. Happy Fourth of July to you, too.'

'Yes, Nietzsche,' I replied.

A car blasting music, full of laughing teenagers, roared past the restaurant as if to prove my point. An old man seated at a table, waiting to order, shook his head in disapproval.

A waitress wearing an American flag pin on her black shirt came over to him with a notepad.

'When I told my mother about my uncle, she said it didn't happen, and that if I told people it did, I would be labelled impure and disobedient.'

I told Franny that after I left home, my cousin told Ammi that the same thing had happened to her. My cousin said my strength had given her the power to speak up about the Religious Uncle from Florence. It had taken her a year to find the courage. Ammi couldn't take it. She couldn't bear the grief. She couldn't bear the guilt.

'We come from families where they teach us to be quiet,' my voice cracked. 'They believe if we don't speak of grief, it will disappear. Silence solves everything.'

The small bell on the restaurant door dinged. A couple walked in, cheery, laughing, leaning onto each other, blissfully caught up in their own little world.

I slid the sushi tray to the side and sat back in my chair. Franny and I stared at each other like two estranged lovers.

'I never told you this,' she said, 'but one of the times I ran away, I tried to end it all. I was fifteen. There's a bridge over a river in my hometown. One night, I stood there and looked down at the water. I can still remember the way the moonlight reflected on the rippling waves.'

A waitress refilled my glass with water. We paused, waiting for her to smile and leave.

'I had never seen anything so beautiful,' Franny continued. 'I just vaulted over.'

'Who saved you?' I asked.

'I did,' she replied. 'That's the strangest thing. I never learned to swim. But once I hit that freezing water, something came over me. I started to kick. I decided I wanted to live.'

'I've read an Arabic proverb which speaks about this,' I said. 'About throwing yourself into the sea, to see if you die or fight to survive.'

'Sometimes you have to do it all yourself,' she said. 'You have to save yourself. You have to choose to live.'

Franny pointed towards her heart and then her head. Her eyes were pools of icy blue water.

'I know you've forgiven your mother,' she said. 'Now, forgive yourself. You didn't kill her.'

Franny said that I could sleep through it. I could try to run from it. It confronts us daily. After years of repressing, it doesn't really go away. You cannot rinse yourself of the past. It is there in the mornings. In the forests. In the blues and browns of your eyes. In classrooms and coffee dates. You just have to deal with it accompanying you everywhere. The storeroom. Ammi. Dur-e-Shahwar. Franny's life in the trailer near the river. The pain will dilute with time. Let it stay.

'It's not easy, but we could try. I don't know,' Franny said. 'Does it get better? Yes, it does.'

⁂

After dinner, we walked to the parking lot. There was a parking ticket under the wiper of the car and I examined it curiously, as if it were a lottery ticket or a flyer for a new amusement park. I had never parked in one place long enough to receive one. I waved it proudly in the air before Franny. She smiled and rolled her eyes.

We drove to a dollar store and purchased two cans of black and purple spray paint, which we took with us to the high school.

'What should we paint?' Franny asked as we looked at a big red-brick wall next to the staircase to the school doors.

'A girl with wings.'

'A girl with wings it is.'

I told her I had never used spray cans before and didn't know how to paint with them. She said to trust her. After all, she did love art.

We drew as best we could, our vision of a girl with wings. It came out okay. Good enough. The girl had beautiful long hair. The wings were glorious and purple. Dur-e-Shahwar was wearing a purple hoodie the day she died. The graffiti did not encapsulate her beauty or innocence, or those curious eyes I saw at CVS and other places, but it did something else for me. It released me from the grief I had been nurturing. Dur-e-Shahwar was there. In the flesh. All healed. All whole. Reclaimed. And she would stay there on the wall, for at least a little while. Demanding attention from joggers and dog walkers and young lovers and children. And a piece of me would be there, in the small pools of uneven paint where I tested out the can for the first time.

'Magnificent,' Franny remarked in an awed whisper as we stepped away and looked at our creation.

The girl with wings.

'Dur-e-Shahwar,' I said finally, her name a quiet prayer.

I drove to Mr Oat's farm so we could sit by the pond. We lowered the windows on the drive. The wind blew through our hair and I laughed as Franny told a story about a colleague who might be in love with her.

I parked the car under our favourite parking spot, a magnolia tree, and checked to see if the lights in Mr Oat's house were out. They were.

We took off our shoes and dipped our feet in the cool water. I could have sworn a faint mist lifted off my skin when I entered the pool. I felt a release.

The stadium wasn't too far from the main house, so we were able to watch the fireworks from the pond. The sky glowed with crackling clusters and streaks of glittering red, white and blue. We sat back and watched them weave Van Gogh patterns in the dark skies.

I leaned back on my arms and imagined the fireworks—willows, peonies, palms and comets—as soaring spirits, hollering dark shadows and autumn leaves falling down, each explosion a burst of freedom, all the things that had been set free.

Worry Doll

Babar's wife fidgeted with the jammed mailbox key. She twisted it back and forth several times to release it from the clasp of the silver keyhole. It was a vulnerable, humiliating moment. She did not want to run upstairs to call Babar. It made her yearn for Karachi.

Zara remembered the simplicity of tasks in Karachi. Her family never had a mailbox. She had never even met the mailman. She did not know if he made his rounds by motorcycle or bicycle. He usually just rang the bell and handed the mail to the gardener, or else tossed it over the gate. It was that simple to receive mail. Although a few times the newspaper landed in massive puddles left by monsoon storms, soggy mail was preferable to worrying whether a key might break inside a lock. Neither she nor Babar knew how to handle such a situation.

After a few more attempts, Zara freed the key and herself from the mailbox, which she had successfully opened. Inside, she found a scattering of grocery store and AutoZone flyers, which she bunched up into a messy pile. She entered the Escape Apartments building with the mail under her arm, passing under the banner management had displayed.

ESCAPE APARTMENTS: REDEFINING HOME.

NOW LEASING FOR 2018–2019. $650 A MONTH.
ALL UTILITIES INCLUDED.

NO WASHER-DRYER.
MILLER'S LAUNDROMAT NEXT DOOR.

It was the end of June. Summer in College Park, Maryland, was pleasant. There was a softness about it. An easiness. Zara and Babar could take long evening strolls without breaking a sweat. The summer days had been difficult in Pakistan. Temperatures soared. There were long, unannounced power cuts. Hours when the backup power gave out. There was nothing much to do after that but confine yourself to a cool basement or an air-conditioned car and feel sympathy for the rickshaw and tonga drivers who roamed the city looking for rides in the sweltering heat.

No power cuts in Maryland. No hot summer days in Maryland. Zara made a mental note. Where there were blessings here, she made sure to count and cherish them.

Zara walked through the stuffy carpeted hallway and entered Apartment 14, shutting the smudgy white door behind her. The first thing to hit her was the smell. An odourous, heavy smell that made her nose twitch. She shook her head in disapproval.

Babar was sitting on the brown polyester living room carpet. He looked up from his laptop screen and surveyed his wife's sullen face. Her black hair was tied up in an unruly bun. A few stray, frizzy baby hairs hovered near her left ear. She wore black-and-red chequered pajama bottoms and a red university T-shirt that the international student officer had given Babar as a gift. It did not fit him.

Babar shrugged in greeting at Zara, who was by then removing her slippers near the door. She made another mental note: *Buy a shoe rack on the next convenience store trip with Nadira.*

Nadira Sultana and her husband Mahmudul Rahman had moved from Dhaka a year ago. Mahmudul worked at the university's IT services department. Nadira stayed home.

Zara took a long, dramatic whiff of the air inside the apartment. She scrunched her nose in displeasure.

'How is this even possible?' Zara asked, tossing the mail she had gathered on the kitchen counter and gesturing widely at the space.

'How ... is ... this ... even ... possible ... Babar?' She spoke in a slow cadence to make sure Babar registered her grievance.

Babar removed his glasses and rubbed his eyes as he prepared to listen.

'It's like someone washed the carpets with garlic cloves and ginger paste.' Zara set a kettle on the stove for her green tea and opened a kitchen cabinet. 'It's like someone buried leftover biryani somewhere and forgot about it.'

'Ahan.'

'What can we do?' Zara inquired as she took down a new coffee mug from the cabinet and removed the sticky price label from the bottom.

'We do nothing. The rent is good for my GTA salary.' Babar's reply was crisp, his words clipped.

The issue with Apartment 14—the main issue—was the lingering smell. Babar and Zara's new College Park apartment contained a distinct, dominating odour of South Asian cuisine. Pakistani, Indian or Bangladeshi, Zara could not tell. It could be all three mixed together, for all she knew. It was the kind of smell that lingers after months, years of tenants cooking the same kind of food over and over again. When they leave, the new tenants repeat the ritual. Then the smell becomes a tradition, and it goes on to become a legacy, a permanent fixture. Pungent fumes trapped in the curtains and carpet. An add-on that came with the new apartment, like a broken washer-dryer or a parking spot too far from the building. Fine print copy in a newspaper advertisement. Something they had to deal with after they'd signed the lease. No internet trick, scented candle, or incense stick worked.

The same odour, Zara noticed, came from Nadira's apartment, though her neighbour did not seem to mind it. The Rahmans continued to exist with the smell and the sound of their rackety air-conditioning unit. This made Zara feel like her fixation was over the top, excessive.

Babar had once used the phrase 'first-world' to describe Zara's gruelling obsession.

'A first-world problem,' he had said. 'It's a very first-world problem.'

Nadira had offered her own suggestion to Zara once, as the two women rode the bus back from an afternoon trip to the grocery store. 'If the smell bothers you too much, pretend it's not there. Then it will cease to exist. The problem will disappear on its own. Trust me.'

Zara had found Nadira's proposal preposterous, but they were new friends. New friends keep their true emotions veiled for at least some time.

Both Zara and Nadira, who liked to be called Nitu, were on a dependent-spouse visa—which meant they could not work. They merely accompanied their husbands to a new country. They merely existed in a country that wanted their partners, not them. Their friendship, formed on the understanding that they would merely exist together, served to fill the empty hours and days and weeks that stretched on for the duration of the visa.

Babar was a tall man. Tallest in his family. His brothers were only five foot seven, but Babar, at twenty-eight, stood at six feet. When they first met, Zara had noticed his broad shoulders, slightly hunched—a remnant of all those teen years spent slouched in front of a computer playing video games, she would later learn.

Babar and Zara were told by family and friends that they made a good couple. Babar was subdued and driven. Zara was passionate and restless. Opposites attract. She was the one who had asked for his phone number at a ghazal night in college. She was the one who called. They dated for two years after that. She was the one who proposed marriage after she turned twenty-seven and received her master's in mass communication. All their friends in college were getting married, so it seemed like a suitable next step. They had been married for almost a year before they moved to America.

When Babar accepted the PhD admission offer from the University of Maryland, it was a given, an unspoken understanding, that Zara was to go with him. She knew foreign spaces could be cruel, and that Babar would not know how to handle this cruelty. He could not be alone in a cruel space. A five-year PhD program was a long time, and neither could imagine a long-distance marriage. Zara also knew that Babar, who had never washed dishes or ironed a shirt in his life, needed a wife to accompany him. He was raised in an environment where there was always help around—an overwhelming, pampering army of mothers, sisters, wives and house help.

According to Zara's girlfriends in Karachi, the move was not a burden but an opportunity. A blessed chance to live away from interfering in-laws, and away from the noise and pollution of Karachi. Her friends voiced their jealousy, speaking often of the freedom Zara would taste in America. After a while, she began to believe them. She began to hate the city, the way it choked and smothered her. She began to hate the paint in her house and the odd chewing noises her sister-in-law made when she ate dinner and how every day a new person asked her when she would have a baby.

At the time, Zara did not know of a single friend who was unhappy living abroad. Or, she thought, maybe they hid their unhappiness behind Facebook photos. Photos with pumpkins and Christmas trees, with sunny beaches and fireworks and watermelon slices. Zara knew many unhappy women in Karachi. They voiced their unhappiness all the time over brunch and Eid dinners. Tragic family sagas involving mothers-in-law and sisters-in-law, giving up their careers for families, balancing work with domestic life, growing older, changing bodies—the inevitabilities of existence.

Zara sat down on the sofa with a steaming cup of green tea and turned to face Babar.

'What if we ask the landlady ... what's her name?' Zara began. 'Ms Stone? What if we ask Ms Stone to get all the carpets cleaned?'

'Carr. Yvonne Carr.' Babar looked straight at his wife. 'Zara, this building has underpaid, hardworking South Asian grad students and workers. They don't give a rat's ass about carpets and smells. It is a luxury. Fragrance is a luxury.'

Babar was familiar with Zara's tendency to fixate on things. He knew her mind created obstacles, preoccupations—sometimes real, sometimes fictitious—to remain busy. After they married, she had spent three weeks searching for the right colour for their bedroom wall. Eggshell White or the French Canvas or the Grey Mirage? She spent another two decorating her office at the advertising firm in Pakistan where she worked as a public relations manager. She visited art galleries in the city, exhibitions and thesis displays by art colleges until she landed on two good charcoal paintings. She spent another week deciding where she wanted the carpenter to build the bookshelf in their living room. By the window, or at the centre near the television set. Or perhaps in a different room altogether. Now, she had carried her obsessions in a suitcase to America.

Babar said that they had to yield to it all: to the smell, old carpet stains, the small microwave plate in the kitchen, the hand-me-down furniture, taxes, 20 per cent tips, the Trump administration, the next election (even if they couldn't vote), snowy winters, lonely holidays, everything. They had to yield to America because it was not their country. It was not Karachi. There was no extra cash, no family, no friends, no help. They didn't have a garden or a terrace, but they had each other and that should be enough.

'It should be enough, Zara,' he reiterated.

Besides, Babar said, there were so many other things he had to figure out before his teaching job began. Getting a Social Security number. Understanding the bus routes to campus. Copying keys for his shared office. Getting a learner's permit for driving. Looking for an old car on Craigslist.

'How will I pass the time when you begin school and leave me behind?' asked Zara.

This was the first time she had asked him that question, the first time she'd spoken her fears into existence. She did not expect him to have an answer, and even if he did, she knew it would still fall upon her to figure things out for herself. Still, she wanted to release the words into the smelly air, have them linger there with the odour.

'Join a class. Spend time with Nitu. Make new friends. Get a driver's license. Explore new places.' This was her husband's reply.

⁂

By August, Babar's graduate school and Mahmudul's job had started, and Nitu and Zara were spending almost all of their time together.

The young women watched Bollywood films on sunken couches while drinking chai and eating snacks. Zara, who could only make eggs or pasta and had never enjoyed cooking, observed with fascination her new friend's remarkable eagerness to try different recipes for her husband. Aloo baingan. Bhindi masala. Lentil and a special rohu fish dish.

Zara cooked out of necessity and boredom. Nitu made it a hobby, a passionate love affair in a new country.

On afternoons when Nitu was free from her cooking, laundry, and tidying, Zara suggested a change of scenery. After a while, the small apartment began to feel stifling, even though Zara was starting to acclimate (slightly) to the smells. To escape, the young women sometimes went jogging near the apartment complex or on hour-long walks around the neighbourhood, discussing homes and lives, old and new.

'Our husbands work very hard and we don't do much to help,' Nitu said once.

'We do,' Zara had replied. 'We cook, vacuum, and light scented candles when they return from classes and work.'

'Yes, but we don't do much to pay the rent, or tuition, or groceries. It's ... it's expensive here.'

There was a trace of guilt in Nitu's voice as she uttered those words. It was as if she thought of herself as a burden, a freeloader. Zara realized that her friend overcompensated for that guilt by being a dutiful housewife abroad. By making sure her husband had a hot breakfast when he woke up, clean pressed laundry ready for work, and that he returned home every evening to the smell of masala chai.

'Well, it's not our fault, is it?' Zara said. 'The word "dependent" in our visa carries a lot of limits. We can't work. Our husbands knew this when they brought us here. The only way we can work is if we get a student visa, and I'm not willing to study again. Or if we babysit.'

Nitu chuckled. 'If our husbands didn't bring us here, where else would we be?'

Zara did not know how to answer, though she did know that her life in Karachi had been full of colour, and could have been more colourful still. If she and Babar had stayed, she could have kept her PR job, could even have dabbled in journalism after a year or two. She would have had meaning, a purpose beyond sitting in a laundromat with Nitu every week watching underwear and trousers spin round and round in big washing machines. She could have hosted Eid parties with family and weekend brunches with colleagues. She could even have gotten a Siamese kitten. Escape Apartments did not allow pets.

Zara and Nitu were different.

Nitu did not mind living in Maryland for the sake of her husband's dream, while Zara secretly began to resent Babar. Nitu was keen on making America home. She saw a future for her children when she chopped garlic cloves and defrosted chicken. Zara did not know if she wanted children at all.

Still, Zara chose to remain in Nitu's company. The truth was that Zara was terrified of being alone. She was never taught how to be alone. She shared a bedroom with her younger sister growing up and roamed the busy streets of Karachi in groups, climbing into packed rickshaws and chauffeured cars with cousins and college friends. She moved from her father's house to her husband's. There had always been company in her life, and so Nitu's company, however bland, filled that void.

Sometimes Zara wondered if Nitu felt the same, if she herself was merely a suitable substitution for the relationships Nitu once had, and missed. Nitu had been friends with the Indian couple who lived in Apartment 14 before Zara and Babar moved in. It seemed like Nitu had more in common with that housewife, Kavya. They were both in their early thirties, and together they had picked up cooking, knitting, and dance to pass the hours. Their husbands had also been good friends.

'It seems like you miss your old friend,' Zara said to Nitu one evening as she reminisced. They sat in Nitu's living room waiting for their husbands to come home.

'I do, but she changed with time.' Nitu was finishing her third glass of wine. 'She changed in the last months.'

'Changed how?'

'She began drinking a lot.'

Nitu said that Kavya missed her workplace and home. She began missing the city she had long wanted to leave. She applied to a PhD program but was not admitted. She did not try again.

'The answer to everything, Zara, is to remain busy. Always remain busy,' said Nitu. 'Always stay busy so the chaos never enters. Fill your calendar. Cook over the bad apartment smell. Otherwise, you won't survive the snow spells, the holidays, the unforgiving hours. You won't survive the hours.'

Zara paused to reflect on Nitu's words. She then murmured to herself, *The Ballad of the Lost Dependent-Visa Wife.*

Nitu said that the university laid off Kavya's husband in January 2018 due to unannounced budget cuts, and eventually the couple moved to Boulder, Colorado, to live with family who could share some of the financial burden. They left behind fizzling friendships, old furniture, and the smell of food. And because their departure was so serendipitously timed with Babar and Zara's arrival, neither Kavya nor her husband, nor Yvonne Carr, cleaned the apartment thoroughly. The old dependent-spouse-visa wife left behind remnants, fragments, of herself, which Zara kept finding in the nooks and crannies of Apartment 14. Once, she found a burned-out incense stick sleeping on the bedroom windowsill. She came across a chain and pendant of Ganesha underneath the bed when she was vacuuming.

There was a squeezed tube of acne medication and a bottle of melatonin in the medicine cabinet. A printed recipe for an eggplant dish and an unopened packet of garam masala in the kitchen cabinet. An empty bottle of Smirnoff and a crumpled brochure for 'Group Mental Health Counselling for Racial/Ethnic Minorities' under the kitchen sink.

And a small doll, smaller than Zara's index finger, tucked under the old mattress. She studied the little figure. It had a carefully shaped body with bits of stick wrapped in vibrant, frayed fabric scraps and threads of red, green, yellow and blue. Black sewn eyes and a thin red thread for lips completed its face.

It was the strangest thing Zara had found in the apartment.

⁂

By fall, Zara had joined a morning yoga class and began inviting Babar's college friends to house parties. Nitu, Mahmudul, and another Bengali couple who lived in the building came by occasionally for evening tea, wine and talk. Zara also got her learner's permit and practised driving in a blue Nissan owned by Audra, one of Babar's colleagues.

There was finally noise in Zara's life.

Audra was from Fairmont, West Virginia. She and Babar had met through one of their university classes, 'Shakespeare in the Anthropocene'. They both taught composition and rhetoric. During driving lessons, they laughed at inside jokes and department politics and exchanged thoughts on seminar classes, PhD reading list preparations and American politics: the refugee crisis, detention centres, campus carry, school shootings. Zara was often left out as they chatted passionately, so she focused her attention on road signs and potholes. There were many empty roads near the DMV where Zara practised with Babar and Audra. Zara had driven most of her life, but wanted to familiarize herself with the new road rules in America. Babar had his eye on a used red 2012 Toyota RAV4. A Pakistani student in the apartment building was selling the old car ahead of his move back home to Peshawar. Zara wanted to be ready when Babar purchased the car.

Always wear a seatbelt. Stop at the stop sign. Yield to pedestrians. Check the speed limit. Practise parallel parking. Slow down in school zones and neighbourhoods. Be careful of wildlife.

During one of the driving sessions, the trio came across a dead deer on the side of the road. It was a disturbing sight. The dainty creature lay prone with its neck bent and limbs sprawled out, the surrounding road painted dark red with its blood.

During another driving lesson, Zara got distracted by a truck with a large Trump MAGA flag fluttering at the back and almost hit a small animal scurrying across the narrow road. She slammed on the brakes, startling the company in the car.

'Jesus, Zara!' Audra exclaimed. 'You never do that.'

'I'm sorry. There was a rabbit or something in the middle of the road ...'

'You can hurt yourself,' Audra continued. 'You should keep your eyes on the road so you can slow down way before the animal comes in front of the car.'

'What if there's no time to stop for an animal?'

'Then it is what it is, unfortunately,' Audra said, shaking her head.

At one of Zara and Babar's house parties, someone had told a story of how they had recently run over a deer on the highway, and how it had not died at the scene but instead limped away into the sea of dark green foliage on the side of the road. The person telling the story had seemed more worried about the damage to the car than about the soon-to-be-dead creature, crying out in the wilderness as its soul left its body. The thought had distressed Zara.

A few people even left the party to go down to the parking lot and examine the wrecked bumper and light.

'Uff,' Babar had said to Zara after the party ended. 'Did you see that car? That was one thing we didn't have to worry about driving in Karachi. Deer pouncing in front of your car.'

In the passenger seat, Audra fiddled with the radio settings, alternating between different stations of static noise. 'When you hit an animal, you have to keep going, sadly,' she said. 'That's the way it is. Or else a car could rear-end you, or you could skid on the ice if the roads are frozen.'

'And don't look back,' Babar added from the backseat.

⁂

When Babar bought the red Toyota for Zara, her compressed world expanded a little bit. She drove around town with Nitu. They went to the Indian grocery store all the way on the other side of town. They went to yoga class, new cafés, and the farmers' market on Sundays.

On days when Nitu was not interested in going anywhere, Zara ventured out alone. Staying inside the apartment complex depressed her. Just as she was growing used to the smell of her new home, she sensed a new smell taking its place. A stronger, more pungent smell of rotten fruits and burnt milk that Babar did not notice, or worse, did not mind.

Once, Zara drove to the liquidation sale of a historic hotel in the middle of town. She felt terrible that a ninety-three-year-old hotel was closing, so she bought a ladle as a souvenir. On another afternoon, she went to explore a potter's field she had found online through a blog named *Fearful Locations in Maryland*. It was a little outside town. She concealed the solitary escapade from Babar because she knew he would reprimand her for driving out too far by herself, without having a driver's license yet.

On another cold evening, she dragged Babar to a vigil outside City Hall in the wake of the Pittsburgh synagogue shooting.

One day after Zara dropped Babar off at the campus for his classes, she returned home and opened the mailbox. Stuffed inside was a black-and-white flyer for the opening of an Artisans' Fair Trade store not too far from Escape Apartments. She convinced Nitu to go with her.

They roamed around, wide-eyed, in the antique store crammed with dusty, dainty-flowered washbasins and Victorian mahogany cabinets. Unopened Coca-Cola bottles from the eighties and baskets full of porcelain and plastic dolls. They checked out the jhumka earrings from Rajasthan, handmade dolls from Guatemala, dreamcatchers from Nepal and chindi baskets from Bangladesh. To Zara's dismay, the fair-trade section had nothing from Pakistan.

'Look at this! How cute!' Nitu picked up the tiny handmade Guatemalan doll from a basket near the cash counter.

It was the same doll Zara had found in Apartment 14. There was a chindi basket full of them. All two inches long, sleeping in green, yellow and red woven pouches.

Nitu read the description tag aloud. 'It's called a worry doll. You're supposed to tell her all your woes, keep her underneath your pillow, and she will absorb all your worries by morning.'

'How does she breathe underneath a pillow?' Zara laughed at her own silly joke.

Nitu snickered to humour her.

Zara trailed behind Nitu and picked up another worry doll from the basket. She took it out of its pouch and laid the tiny thing in the middle of her palm.

She observed the doll's colourful skirt, which, according to the tag, was made of leftover textiles and wool. Zara rubbed the thin fabric between her thumb and index finger. The doll had no expression.

'Too much pressure on the little thing, no?' Zara said. 'She's supposed to listen and soak up all your grief.'

She looked at the price tag.

'Two dollars. A doll that will take away all your grief is worth two dollars,' Nitu said.

Zara tossed the tiny thing back into the basket.

The Thanksgiving break in late November brought howling wind, sleet, and road salt. An unfamiliar world unraveled before Zara, who had only seen snow in movies as a romanticized, glorious affair.

The town became quiet and empty. Mahmudul and Nitu drove down to Arlington to meet family. Zara's yoga teacher travelled to Miami.

As time elapsed, silence brewed between Zara and Babar. He spent most of his days studying and grading, or asking Zara to drive him to his office, the library, or a peer's house. Beyond that, there were few conversations to be had. There was no family gossip or news, and Babar seemed uninterested in hearing about the plots of the movies Zara was watching, or the books she was reading. Her days were cloaked in dullness. Instead of speaking to Babar, Zara began speaking to the worry doll she had found in the apartment. She held the doll in her palm and whispered to it, like a child confiding in their best friend on a playground. She spoke about the weather, her mother and the pink dahlias in her childhood garden back home.

Zara and Babar never had much in common, but that didn't seem to matter in Karachi with all the noise and commotion. They led lives which were separate yet tied through family and mutual friends. Now he was transforming into someone quiet but hungry for new surroundings, bursting with insatiable academic curiosity and hope for new beginnings. And Zara was like a bird, crooning, flying around, looking for twigs, sticks, leaves and grass to build a nest somewhere in an unwelcoming forest.

Five months had gone by since Babar started teaching, and Zara had yet to find her footing. Her spirit had never been so empty, so austere, without the tumultuous disorder of daily life in Karachi. Whether that was a good or bad thing, she still didn't know. Whether she was languishing or resurfacing, she still didn't understand. There was noise in her life, yes, but it was a faint noise that faded in and out, never constant, never fulfilling.

Their relationship was becoming one of lukewarm love and convenience. A marriage that had begun to fall into predictable patterns. A relationship that had to be sustained in bad weather and governance, in a quaint town on a snowy holiday, in a small apartment with an odour which grew progressively worse with time.

It was the right kind of marriage, her mother told her over the phone.

The comfortable kind. The normal kind. Perhaps the only kind her mother knew.

✦

The morning before Thanksgiving, Zara was cleaning the living room window with a wet newspaper. The glass made a squeaking sound as she tried to remove a smudge. As she concentrated on a particularly stubborn part of the stain, an idea birthed in her mind.

Babar was working on his laptop, clacking away at the keyboard.

'Let's do it,' she said, turning around and looking at Babar. 'Let's have a Thanksgiving meal tomorrow, just the two of us. I'll cook. All the traditional American Thanksgiving dishes. I'll follow recipes from the internet.'

'Oh, okay,' Babar replied, not sure why Zara wanted to drown in so much kitchen work.

'It might feel less lonely,' she added. They had not planned to do anything for Thanksgiving, and with all of their friends away, Zara was beginning to feel as though she was going about things all wrong.

'Lonely? Are you lonely?' Babar's eyebrows knitted. 'Are we lonely?'

'You know what I mean. It's the holiday season,' Zara said. 'If we were home, we would be surrounded by friends and family, like everyone else.'

'We don't have a holiday season in Pakistan, Zara,' Babar said. 'This is our first. We don't have anything to compare it with.'

'We have Eid and we've seen Thanksgiving and Christmas in movies,' she said. 'The laughing families, big parties, awkward confrontations and the leftovers. No one mentions the Pakistani couple who never gets invited anywhere.'

Babar fell silent for a few moments. His mind was still stuck on the word she had used earlier. Lonely.

He told Zara that he did not understand what she meant by that. He had seen her with Nitu and other friends. He had seen her smiling and laughing in bars and at parties.

Zara had never mentioned loneliness to Babar. Or unhappiness. Or bitterness. Or even jealousy when he spent time with Audra or suggested that Zara take up more of Audra's hobbies, like hiking.

'Are you lonely here?' he asked, still perplexed.

Zara did not reply; instead, she began dusting the bookshelf. She picked up Kavya's little worry doll from the shelf and looked at it. She stroked its blank face with her thumbs as if trying to wake it up.

'I don't know what I am here,' Zara replied, grimly. 'Sad? Lonely? Happy? I don't know. I'm just here with you because this is where I have to be ... should be.'

Babar slapped his laptop shut. 'Let's do it, if that makes you happy.'

'Do what?' Zara asked, dazed. 'Oh yes! The Thanksgiving dinner!' She quickly set about making an ingredient list.

'By the way, what's this little thing you keep holding?' Babar called from the living room.

'It's a worry doll.'

'What does it do?'

'The same things all regular dolls do. You play with it, keep it wherever you want, and it doesn't talk back.'

Babar did not reply.

⁂

The autumn-themed grocery store aisles were a cornucopia of baked bread, pumpkin pies and discount turkeys. Children scurried through the crammed, narrow passageways with trolleys. Zara and Babar shopped and drove back to Escape Apartments with a frozen chicken, potatoes, yams and other ingredients. On the side of the road, they saw the same dead deer they had seen weeks earlier, during Zara's driving lesson with Audra.

It was much smaller now, shrivelled, yet still it rested just as before, unaddressed, neglected, on a blanket of snow.

'You'd expect they'd clean up dead things in America and not bury them under snow,' Babar said.

Zara sped past the creature. She couldn't look into its dead eyes. They were open, frozen in a blank stare, implicating the vehicles that drove by, as if praying that someone would scoop it up and bury it somewhere with dignity, somewhere where crows, coyotes or other scavengers could consume it and erase it from this earth.

The Thanksgiving meal was pleasant. There were no centrepieces but there were scented candles. There was no stuffed turkey but there was a roasted chicken. There were no friends or family, just the two of them eating by the flickering candlelight. For a while there was silence, punctuated by the sounds of clinking silverware on the ceramic plates Zara had brought from Karachi. This was interrupted by bursts of small talk about how well everything was cooked. Then, they spoke about many things, the marvellous and the not so marvellous.

The marvellous: Babar said Audra wanted to get chickens for her backyard and had asked for their help constructing a chicken coop. Zara did not care for it.

The ordinary: Zara said her hair wouldn't stop falling out.

Maybe there was something in the water, something her body didn't like. Babar said he hadn't noticed anything, neither her thinning hair nor the newness in the American water.

The conversation veered towards Babar's academic pursuits, and he explained to Zara the world of metaphysical poets and the use of iambic pentametre. She nodded along, pretending to understand.

⁂

When Nitu returned from her holiday in Virginia, she had news. She was four months pregnant and deliriously happy. She had spoken to Mahmudul about possibly moving to a cleaner, two-bedroom apartment once the baby arrived.

Zara did not want her friend to move but she pursed her lips and stayed quiet. Nitu's happiness was not to be jeopardized by her own selfish desire.

Over the next two weeks, Nitu suggested that Zara start thinking of having a baby herself. Nursing a baby might help her nurse the void she felt in Maryland.

Zara often looked sad, Nitu remarked.

'Think about it,' Nitu said every time she saw Zara in the hallway or the parking lot, believing that if she spoke the words often enough, Zara would eventually cling to the idea. Nitu started spending more time inside the apartment and less time outside. She no longer wanted to go to the store, or for a jog, or to artisan fairs. Zara felt the noise in her life beginning to ebb away. She began talking more to the worry doll. After Babar left for work, she would hold it up to her chest and admit all kinds of secret things:

I wonder what my mother and sister are doing right now in Pakistan.

I used to love my office back home.

The smell here won't leave me alone.

If I cook enough, will I replace the old smell with a new?

I don't like this Audra girl.

Instead of making a baby as Nitu advised, Zara got her driver's license on her first attempt. She took long walks around the campus despite the sleet, salt and snow. She made two new friends at yoga who made her sign up for weekend Zumba classes. She began hoarding frozen pasta, pizza and vegetables for an oncoming blizzard in January. She had heard about it on the car radio. She asked her yoga friends what the difference was between a snowstorm and a blizzard.

'I think a blizzard is like the mother of a snowstorm,' she told Babar.

Zara even called the Department of Transportation to ask about the delay in removing the forgotten deer carcass. It still had not fully decayed and the low temperatures kept it from rotting. Forever preserved. Forever still. Forever dead. She saw it every time she took the car out.

Zara remained suspended somewhere between the slush of College Park and the pollution of Karachi, somewhere between the lonely days inside Apartment 14 and the carefree times she'd take her bicycle out on a street in Karachi as a teenager. Somewhere between the dull hours on Nitu's couch and the reimagined dusty moments in her grandmother's sunny courtyard, and somewhere between the smell of food Kavya had left behind and the new smell that was beginning to take its place.

One afternoon, Zara sat with Nitu in her apartment and watched a 1955 Bollywood film. They watched actors Raj Kapoor and Nargis lock eyes and lip-synch to a love song as they shared an umbrella in the pouring rain.

Zara was waiting on Babar, who had promised to return home as soon as his lecture ended. They were to go to a famous taco shop in Baltimore before dark. Thirty minutes after he was supposed to arrive, he called to say that Audra wanted help with a paper that was to be submitted the next day.

Tacos could wait. The paper could not.

Zara cut the call before her husband could placate her with another promise.

Anger boiled inside her. She thought about her husband, how he treated her no better than a dead worry doll, buried beneath a pillow and forgotten, her existence serving no purpose but to absorb his sorrows and smile for his ambitions.

She pictured Audra's face, her coquettish laughter at parties, her blonde hair in a ponytail, her blue eyes wide as Babar revised the paper in her office ...

'Let's go have tacos,' Zara said loudly to Nitu, shaking off the intrusive thoughts. She decided that she would not sit around waiting for Babar to arrive.

'All the way to Baltimore?'

'It is only a forty-minute ride.'

Zara told Nitu that she could drive easily. It wasn't snowing anymore and the roads were safe.

The reluctant Nitu sat in the passenger seat and strapped on a seatbelt, the fabric expanding over the new bulge in her stomach.

'I wish I could have a margarita,' she laughed as Zara revved up the engine and began driving out of the apartment parking lot.

Zara merged onto the highway and soon realized the roads were slicker than she had anticipated. There was no sun. There had been no sun for over a week. Just dark, morbid skies, foggy roads and the plangent whistling of cold, unnerving wind.

Be prepared. Use your headlights. Add antifreeze.

Zara recalled the notes she had made about driving in harsh winter months.

Stay home if possible. Avoid driving unless absolutely necessary.

Nitu kept chatting throughout the ride. She wondered what was so special about those tacos in Baltimore. She wondered if she and Mahmudul could afford a townhouse near the arboretum once the baby arrived. She asked Zara what her plans were for the new year.

Zara said nothing. Her mind remained consumed by other things. Random things. Bizarre memories. She thought about the day she married Babar. She had spent too much on a wedding dress. She wondered why she would do that for an event that lasted only five hours.

If she had waited a year to learn that Babar had been admitted to grad school, would she still have married him? What would she have done? Was she being ungrateful about living in America? Was she not trying hard enough to love the place, love her marriage? Were all her worries too first-world, as Babar had said?

There had been love, once. But not enough for Zara to set herself on fire and burn day after day for his passion. She felt like a horrible wife. A useless worry doll. A worry doll burdened with her own problems.

'Selfish, selfish woman,' Zara whispered.

She held the steering wheel as the car picked up speed, her knuckles turning white around the leather sheaf.

Selfish, ungrateful woman. These were the words she knew her mother, friends and neighbours would say behind her back if she returned to Karachi after leaving her husband.

There were three options, Zara thought: drink away and be silent like Kavya, have a child and buy a townhouse like Nitu, or remain still and power through until there was a new road to be found. If there was a new road.

Zara pushed down on the accelerator.

'We are going pretty fast, don't you think?' Nitu asked, glancing over at Zara.

'It's fine,' Zara responded, still quietly seething in anger. 'We want to get there before the taco shop closes.'

'Please, you're making me nervous,' Nitu said, her voice wavering slightly. She reached up and pulled at her seatbelt to tighten it.

'Don't worry!' Zara sped up slightly, and the world around the car became a blur of colours.

Suddenly, a spot appeared in the distance, getting closer and closer.

'Oh God! There's something on the road!' Nitu cried out. 'Slow down! Slow down! For God's sake, slow down!' It was a deer. Zara could make out the frail brown body, but there was not enough time or distance to slow down or slam on the brakes. It was coming up fast now.

'I don't want to kill it!' Zara screamed.

'Don't stop now! You cannot stop now!' Nitu cried.

Zara did not listen. She swerved the car. The wheels screeched as she narrowly missed the deer. The car spun two times on the freezing road.

Nitu shrieked and bowed her head, bracing for impact.

Everything was unfocused, violent and rushed.

The car slid down a slope and crashed into a ditch, just a few feet away from a bare, snow-clad tree. For a few seconds, neither woman moved. After a while, they looked at each other and then ahead at the windshield.

Zara's heart pounded as she clutched the steering wheel. She let go, lay back in her seat, unstrapped her seatbelt and buried her face in her hands, trying to collect herself.

There was a whirl of unbridled rage from Nitu's side. 'Are you insane?! Are you crazy, Zara?!' Nitu burst into tears. 'Who drives so fast on such roads? I told you to slow down!'

Zara looked out her window to see if she could spot the animal, alive, safe, standing somewhere near them.

'I told you to slow down!'

Zara could not see anything but snow and trees.

'Are you listening to me?' Nitu said. 'Oh God, what are we going to do now? Whom do we call?'

Zara's mind was elsewhere. She put on her red winter coat and opened the car's glove compartment to find her mittens. It had started to snow again. Large flakes landed softly on the windshield and the ground around the car.

Zara got out of the car. The cold, piercing wind sliced her face. Her boots kept digging deep in the snowy ground. It was a peril to walk in five inches of snow.

'What are you doing?' Nitu hollered through the open door, leaning towards the driver's seat.

'I have to find it,' Zara said. 'What if I injured it? What if the deer got hurt?'

Nitu kept talking, telling her she was crazy, that she did not hit the deer. It must have escaped. Zara did not believe her. Zara did not want the animal to die slowly, painfully, in some cold woods.

'How will it breathe underneath all that snow?'

Zara swam in a swirl of madness. She walked against the powerful winds, shin-deep into snow, looking for deer tracks or scurries. She stood on the highest rock she could find and looked around.

Nothing. Absolutely nothing. Just snowy trees. Endless peaks of white. Boundless spaces of white.

As Zara began her walk back to the car, she fell on her knees. She sank deeper into the ground and lay on her back in the snow with her arms sprawled out like a child making snow angels, like the dead deer on the side of the road, like the small worry doll hidden underneath the mattress.

Zara looked up at the dark skies and watched the flakes fall down slowly. Onto her face. Into her hair. Onto her red coat and gumboots. She finally returned to the car and slammed the door shut.

Nitu cried and spoke about how Zara was too much for her, her overbearing friendship, her adventures, her restlessness, while Nitu herself wanted something different from this new life. She was trying.

Nitu's tongue was fiery and fierce. Her words poured out without trepidation. Zara did not want to look at her. Did not want to confront or comfort her, or admit that maybe she was right. Maybe she could have just pushed through and crushed the animal—or better, just stayed home and cried herself to sleep over missed tacos and Babar's attention.

Zara let Nitu wail and call 911.

In her peripheral vision, Zara sensed a brown shape move towards her window. She looked closely through the frosted glass and saw a hazy image. A deer. Zara rubbed furiously at the condensation on the window to get a better look.

There it was, staring at her. A beautiful, unscathed deer. It had to be the same one she had just saved. Zara knew this to be true. The animal touched its nose to the glass.

Zara raised her hand and the deer moved back a little in fright. It stood still and relaxed as Zara touched the glass with her fingers, as if trying to stroke it for comfort.

A fawn appeared behind the deer, its head bowed and small. They stayed like that, the three of them, staring at each other silently as snow fell all around. Silent in understanding.

Then, in a flash, the deer and the fawn trotted away into the woods and disappeared behind a blanket of trees. The falling snow covered their tracks, as if they had never existed.

'It was a mother,' Zara said.

'What?' Nitu had just ended her call. She cleaned the snot streaming down from her nose with the sleeve of her sweater. 'That deer on the road,' Zara said. 'It was not alone. It was a mama.'

'What?'

Zara's mind was scattered. 'How do we win? How does the worry doll breathe under the pillow?'

Nitu looked at her in confusion, her eyes wide with repulsion. Zara was not helping Nitu's anxiety attack.

'How does she breathe?' Zara asked again.

Nitu lifted her hand to prevent Zara from speaking. She was making no sense.

As they waited for a state trooper to rescue them, Zara tried to turn on the engine for the third time. It sputtered and made a grinding noise.

Minutes stretched on for what felt like an eternity as they sat quietly in the cold, waiting to be saved. Nitu breathed heavily, refusing to look at her friend. Zara's eyes scanned the barren landscape, her mind preoccupied with thoughts of dolls and deer. After a while, the women heard a siren blaring. Nitu opened her door and left Zara alone. She wanted to flag down the car. She was afraid of dying in the middle of nowhere.

After a few moments, an officer knocked at Zara's window. 'Ma'am, open the door. We're here now.'

Zara didn't move. She stayed entombed in the car. 'Ma'am?'

She did not want to go home to Escape Apartments, to Kavya's lingering smell, to the new rotten smell, to the worry doll, to Babar's questions about how she could be unhappy with a car and friends in such a desirable country.

She looked at Nitu sitting inside the officer's car from her rearview mirror. She had stopped crying. Her face was vacant, bland. She was ready to be taken home.

Worry dolls, Zara thought, weary dolls. Buried underneath the malaise. Burying an onslaught of emotions. Buried underneath the lullabies of a good marriage. Chores. Garlic cloves and peppercorns. Laundromats and dryer sheets. Birthday parties in parks with a folding table, cheese boards and cheap wine.

Worry dolls like her and Nitu and Kavya. The unsung heroes. Like the mice in the laboratory or a mother with ten kids in a rural village in Pakistan.

Weary dolls, waiting. Good, biddable, offering women. Pretending to ignore the smell, the sadness, the snowy days, the drifting marriage. Burying everything they feel beneath a pillow, behind ornamental peonies and spider plants. Waiting for a windfall. Chasing a windfall. A stroke of good news. Anything to make the day. Maybe a baby that saves a relationship. A new Pakistani recipe that saves the fifteen dollars that was to be handed to a pizza deliveryman instead. The feeling when a visa application is finally accepted, the feeling when a customs officer behind glass at the airport counter hands back your passport and says, Welcome to America.

Everyone wants to go to America. Everyone seems happy in America.

⁂

The women sat in the officer's car. He talked all through the jolting drive.

'I'm surprised the air bags didn't deploy,' he said. 'Maybe that's because it's an old car.'

Nitu remained quiet. She had resolved to ignore Zara forever.

'Where are you ladies from?' asked the officer.

'College Park, Maryland,' spoke Nitu.

'No, where are you really from?'

'College Park, Maryland,' said Nitu, again.

⁂

Back in the apartment, Babar said many things. Many comforting things. Many things to make Zara realize she had risked three lives that day for tacos.

The following week was slow. On Monday, she went out for a walk alone and counted all the churches in the neighbourhood. There were five. On Tuesday, she asked Babar what vegan really meant, and later in the day she called the landlady to scold her about the conditions in Escape Apartments. On Wednesday, she stood by the window looking at ongoing traffic and wondering how far she could drive with her international license. On Thursday, she began to miss Nitu, but not enough to knock at her door. On Friday, she whispered all her worries to the doll before going to bed. On Saturday, she called animal control again and once more informed them about the dead deer on the side of the road. She went to watch two men take it away. From the confines of her car, she observed them clearing out the road, and the emptiness that followed. From the car seat, as she stared at the now empty space, she dreamt of another life. A life where she and Babar spent the days sitting in their living room in Karachi, walls painted a perfect Grey Mirage, a bookshelf full of books by the window. And by Sunday, she knew it was over.

Ruby

My mother was not one woman. She was two. Though I did not discover this until my father died.

The first woman, Rubina, was a forlorn figure, a pious and hardworking mother and wife who took care of her thirteen-year-old daughter and ailing husband without complaint. She tended to the house as her husband squandered money on gambling and cigarettes. She paid the bills by cleaning bathrooms and washing clothes in big bungalows. The obedient wife, the self-sacrificing woman, Rubina played her role in the marriage for the sake of family and honour. She paid the electric and gas, took me to different doctors for my ugly arm, and boiled water on the stove for the house during the rough winter months.

When my father died from a heart attack, Rubina organized a great funeral. She arranged two daigs of pulao—heaping pots of spicy rice cooked with tender chicken pieces and bowls of raita with fresh yogurt, spices, cucumber and mint leaves for all the mourners who came for the free lunch. I watched Rubina sob softly into her dupatta as four men, pallbearers, lifted the charpoy with my father's dead body wrapped in white, and walked together in a procession to the Christian graveyard where my grandparents were buried. As Rubina cried, she lifted her hands to her face, exposing pinkish-white patches on her skin, recent symptoms of a strange illness she had contracted earlier that year. The patterns had spread to her left foot, her back, and now just above her lip, a spot which she covered with thick orange lipstick whenever we went out. A skin specialist at a government hospital told us she had vitiligo, a disease triggered by grief and stress.

'Your father has left on my skin a reminder of our bad marriage,' Rubina said to me once while we sat on a patch of grass outside the hospital. Father was still alive then, though he had suffered a stroke. The doctors put two expensive stents in his heart to keep him alive. The cardiologist told him that he must stop smoking if he wanted to live. He kept smoking anyway.

'I will live under a shadow if he dies today,' Rubina continued. 'These spots will mark me forever.' She picked at a blade of grass as I worked on my social studies homework beside her.

'It doesn't look that bad, Amma,' I said, looking up from my notebook. 'No one even notices it.'

I was trying to write the names of Pakistan's national flower and animal for class, before moving on to read a chapter on the Indus Valley Civilization, but Rubina kept distracting me, wallowing as she plucked her eyebrows with a silver tweezer in the sunlight, examining the white patches on her lips and hands. She was a crumbling mess. A muddle of melancholy, of uneven patches, hypertrophic scars and weathered lines on her skin.

'People do. They notice everything, Kaki,' she replied. 'Even the children, they aren't innocent little things anymore. They're cruel and vile just like their parents. Say whatever cruel shit comes to their mind.'

I did not respond. I feared agreeing would only hurt her more, but I knew she was right. People did notice. They spoke about everything and everyone. Other people's luck, good and rotten. Other people's miseries and misfortunes. Especially the miseries and misfortunes. At the funeral, between the sobbing and the silence, I overheard neighbours and relatives chatting about my father's sinful habits, wondering if Jesus would forgive him in the afterlife, wondering if God would heal Rubina's spreading vitiligo and my ugly, polio-affected arm.

'Who will marry Kanwal when she grows up?' asked Rehana auntie, a neighbour. 'Poor Kaki, who would marry Kaki?'

I would be lying if I said the thought had never troubled me. The look of my arm, so grotesque and abnormal, coiled like a serpent, pained me. The deformity marked me out in schools and bazaars, around flea markets and at bus stops. Rubina swore that real beauty came from within, but I knew this to be a lie. People will always love beautiful hair, slender fingers with painted nails and chiselled jaws over a beautiful soul. None of the Bollywood heroines looked like me. None of the women I saw at the bus stop looked like me. I saw myself only in the man who begged for money at the main traffic signal near Kalma Chowk. When cars stopped at the red light, he approached, rapping on windows, pleading, dancing his arm around, dangling it for show.

I hid my own arm underneath a scarf.

'Sometimes life becomes easier when you shut your brain and do not think,' I remember Rubina telling me once. Rubina was a master at shutting away her emotions. Floating through the day, a million miles away. Waiting for Abba to grow old and die so our lives could begin. A clean slate.

At the funeral, an older woman leaned over towards Rehana auntie and, in a coarse whisper, asked, 'Is there a surgery for polio? Or will she remain damaged for the rest of her life?'

The rest of my life. I tucked those words away as the women at the funeral moved on to discuss other things. How would Rubina be able to pay for hospital bills, my school fees, moving expenses, the expensive rickshaw rides to Sacred Heart Cathedral for Sunday services? How could one woman who scraped shit out of toilet bowls with Dettol and cleaned mould from kitchen tiles do all those difficult things without a husband? They did not know the answer, and neither did I.

But I would soon find it.

⌘

The day we buried my father, I met Ruby. As they lowered his casket, she emerged, like an Amaltas tree in full bloom, awakened after a morbid season with golden clusters blooming. Radiant with a new hope. A new life.

Ruby was a fire-starter. An escape artist. A magician. A liar. A lover. A creature without God. A creature with enormous wings, frightening like Gabriel's, who covered the horizon from end to end when he sailed up into the skies. Ruby, too, could, in an instant, beat her wings and soar away from those that would harm her. Taint her. Stifle her. Ruby knew just when to leave things behind, while Rubina withered in plain sight. Stewed in silence and sabr—patience—the way good women in bad marriages should do.

Having borne years of quiet, pent-up resentment, small injustices that dug away at her soul, Ruby had awoken.

At the funeral, we buried more than my father. My mother made sure to bury Rubina in the ground with him. She was done with that part of her life.

That hollow shell of a woman.

✦

The next time we moved homes was in April, thirteen months after my father's death. The rent for our old quarter was too high, and we had found a more suitable home for the two of us. A place that did not reek of the past, his presence, the funeral and Rubina's quiet desperation. Without a husband, Ruby was a free woman. And I was a half-orphan. To our old neighbours and distant relatives, we were pitiable, wretched things, more so than before, without a man's protective shadow around us.

Ruby was eager to begin anew. A few weeks after Abba died and the steady stream of mourners slowed to a trickle, she gave away his old clothes to the milkman. She cut ties with his family. She trimmed her hair and coloured it a deep burgundy. 'Ruby,' she called herself. She cackled loudly. She flirted with men in shops. She sometimes pretended I didn't exist, that she was just a woman, unburdened by a child.

When she wanted to sleep in, when she asked that I take myself to school, I acquiesced. When she bought a new shawl with the money we were saving for my shoes, I said nothing. I did not want to cast a shadow over her happiness, an unfamiliar happiness I had never seen before.

I didn't like the new mohalla, our new community. Rehmat Nagar, it was called. The neighbourhood of mercy. An odd name, I thought. The place was covered in paper. All around there were signs, black-and-white notices, advertisements printed on cheap white canvas and plastered on flaking walls, shop doors and electric poles. Advertisements for English classes and appointments with agents who could help people escape to a better life in Canada. Posters of a morose-looking politician humbly begging for votes and promising to change the city. Another advertisement for a faith healer, a deeply spiritual man who promised good fortune and romantic success, vowing to ward off evil eyes for an affordable price.

But there was one notice in particular, a warning notice, which troubled me. I spotted it the day we moved in. The notice was written in Urdu. I read it aloud to Ruby as we unlocked our apartment for the first time: *Only Muslims can live in these quarters.*

Ruby was unperturbed.

'Only Muslims can live in these quarters,' I whispered again.

She stuffed her gold cross into the crevice of her bosom and opened the tin door. The flimsy thing swung wildly and slammed against a wall.

'Then, we will be Muslims for the next few months,' she said.

I was learning that Ruby always found a way to survive.

I stood reluctantly at the threshold of our new dwelling, holding a bundle of clothes in my right arm, refusing to enter. A little down the alley, I saw a girl close to my age wave at me and disappear inside a house.

'Aajao, come on now, Kaki,' Ruby coaxed as she entered the house. Her new friend Ghulam Rasool, the carpenter, was arriving later in a loader truck to bring up our furniture. They had met several weeks earlier at a shoe store.

I stepped inside the courtyard and looked around. It was a one-bedroom, with a latrine toilet and a loose, trembling washbasin, and a small outdoor kitchen with corrugated metal roofing. There were dusty, empty juice boxes and packets of Top Pops chips in the courtyard which the neighbours' children must have tossed over the low walls of the vacant house. We had lived in worse places before. One summer, before my father died and at the peak of a scorching heat wave, we lived in a cramped servants' quarter on a rooftop infested with mosquitoes and lizards. In the dead of winter, the three of us lived with a gardener and his family in the one-bedroom servants' quarter of a bungalow. There were seven children and the space was crowded. They scribbled on the walls with pencils and hid my school bag for fun. None of them went to school. They asked me to recite the first qalma. They told me I must become a Muslim if I planned to go to heaven. They said my arm was deformed because I was a Christian. It was God's wrath, and if they touched me, their arm would be deformed too. I was infected. I passed the days coiled under a blanket.

When the gardener's children got pink eye from their cousins and gave it to me, I did not say a word. I suffered the sickness they gave to me in silence. The only person I confided in was my mother.

'Talk to Jesus, cry to him and tell him you're hurt,' Rubina had said at the time. 'No one else.'

I wondered how much Jesus's heart could take.

She knew the cost of retaliation. She told stories of neighbours, friends, distant relatives, all punished for being Christian. I understood, even at that age, that we were to live our lives as particles of dust, forgotten in quiet corners, beneath shoes. We barely existed for Abba. We barely existed for our relatives. We barely existed at all.

⌘

After the move to Rehmat Nagar, we spent the next few days unpacking our belongings. Cotton shirts, old sweaters, shawls we had acquired over the years. Donations from Ruby's former mistresses. She had worked for five different women in the thirteen months since Abba died, though none had liked her enough to keep her on as a maid. Some accused her of stealing milk and eggs from the fridge, while others complained of her sharp tongue and bad attitude. I never asked Ruby about the eggs or the fine curries she sometimes brought home, or about the loose change she would fish out of her bra at the end of her shifts. When our eyes met, there was no trace of shame. She reminded me of the electricity bill and the notebooks and pencils I needed for school. These were desperate times. Getting by was viewed as a quiet form of justice.

'Even if we take a few rupees from these rich women, it won't matter,' Ruby told me as we unpacked. She had taken out a small wallet full of coins and loose change she had collected from various dressers and end tables. 'These people will always be rich. They'll always have big houses with good clothes, food to eat, air conditioners ... nobody watches over the poor. Dead or alive, no one watches over us.'

'Not even Jesus?' A pause.

'Sometimes I wonder.'

Ruby grabbed a straw broom and began sweeping the bedroom, stirring up clouds of dust.

'What will happen if someone in the colony finds out we're Christian?' I asked, coughing. 'What will they do?'

I knew the answer. I had lived the answer. Many times we were asked to vacate, relocate, scram, by unfeeling landlords with hard-set jaws and gruff voices.

'Kaki, for now just remain quiet,' cautioned Ruby. 'This is temporary.'

She told me that the lie was to be echoed until she found us a cheaper place to live, closer to school or to her work. She had recently been hired to clean for a woman in a bungalow at Upper Mall next to the grand, red-bricked Lahore Museum and the General Post Office building. Ruby was content, so I had to be content.

'What about this Jesus calendar?' I reached into my bag and pulled out a rolled-up calendar with a colourful picture of Jesus Christ, given to us at church. I spun the calendar so Ruby could look into Jesus's blue eyes, and Jesus could look back into hers.

'Jesus doesn't need to be hung on walls,' she replied. 'He should reside in hearts.'

Her tone was unconvincing. There was a knock at the door. Ghulam Rasool had arrived with the remainder of our things. Ruby washed her face and fixed her hair. I watched her skip across the courtyard to open the door for the new man she would outgrow before the end of the week.

⌘

Ruby began dating three months after Abba died. A small part of me, the selfish part, was relieved when Abba died. I thought that with him gone, my mother would finally become mine. That she would take me to parks and bazaars. To the shops and the family village. Her preoccupation with Abba, with house chores, and then suddenly with the funeral, had kept her away from me for years. Away from herself, too. After Abba's death, I assumed I would take up the space he'd left behind.

But Ruby did not want to live life as before. All that life and circumstance had stolen in her childhood and youth, she wanted back. She bathed in the light of a new life, of new liberty, charting her own territory to become the woman she had always wanted to be. She filled that empty space with new men, new lovers, new adventures.

These men showered Ruby with presents. Ghulam Rasool gifted her a Nokia 150. Akbar, a security guard at a wealthy English school, bought her bangles. From someone else, she received a Khaadi cotton shalwar kameez.

There were other presents too, presents of the heart. Akbar took Ruby on picnics and recited poetry among the blooming marigolds. For days afterwards, Ruby recited those lovely words as she walked through the city, through markets, through the house.

'Tear down the mosque, the temple, everything your eye can see. But don't ever break a human heart. For that is

where God lives. What beautiful words, Kaki. Maybe he's the one. He's not married. And he isn't asking me to become a Muslim like that zookeeper Sharif did. Do you remember Sharif?'

I did. Sharif always smelled of animal shit and bird feathers. I did not believe that losing him was a great loss. I did not believe any man's disappearance was a loss. Not even Abba's for that matter.

Ruby held Akbar's poem close to her heart and whispered the lines to herself in the quiet hours of the morning. Weeks later, as we were running errands, she saw those same poetic words written on the back of a truck carrying bricks to a construction site.

'The bastard copied Bulleh Shah,' Ruby spat. Her face flooded with shame and the shadows of dashed hopes. 'You can't trust men with anything, Kanwal, I'm telling you. They're just good for free ice cream and mobile credit.'

I knew this already but still I nodded along, listening intently.

'When these men are broken, there's always someone to pick them up, to lift them up and shake off the dust,' she went on for days. 'Their mothers, their sisters, their wives, they will take care of these men. Who looks after a broken woman? No one comes to collect the pieces of a broken woman. She picks herself up, glues herself back together while taking shit from everyone, walks around like a damaged mosaic, a patchwork of broken things, and still suffers through life.'

I secretly relished Ruby's broken heart. With every disappointment, I drew her in closer. Smoothed her hair while she cried, whispered soft, kind words, reminded her that I was there for her, I would always be there for her.

In the wake of her sorrow I became her foundation. In the old days, Rubina would collapse before me in a heap after one of Abba's tirades, violent or not. In those desperate moments she bore her soul, and I felt loved. Ruby, on the other hand, was guarded. Poised. Fearless. In sadness, I missed Rubina. Her days of disillusionment and vulnerability brought me great joy. I mattered then.

⁂

Out of all of Ruby's men, out of all the carpenters, the janitors, the pharmacy salesmen, the nurses and the tuition teachers, Samuel Messiah was my favourite. He was a good man. A kind man. A Christian man.

We met him by accident, only a week after we moved to Rehmat Nagar, when our rickshaw collided with his rackety, second-hand Hero motorbike. We crashed in an explosion of thin grey-white clouds and kicked up dirt, and in a fury Samuel pulled our driver out of his seat by the collar and began screaming obscenities. Ruby lunged forward from the back passenger seat, where I sat terrified and held Samuel's wrist in a tight grip.

'You want to punish a poor man who drives a rickshaw?' she asked. Her stare cut through him. 'Blame the government who put up busted traffic lights on a busy chowk!'

As a child I could not understand what happened next, but I now know that in the cannonade of screeching cars, motorbike horns, hawkers, and sweaty, cursing van drivers, Samuel fell for the passionate woman with fire in her eyes.

Ruby was magic for young men, even with her vitiligo and her chequered history. Samuel let the rickshaw man go, but he did not let go of Ruby.

⌘

We had always moved often, and so my relationships with people and places were paper thin, easily ripped up and discarded with every subsequent upheaval. I developed a habit of keeping my belongings in one place and my bag half packed at all times, a habit of keeping my eyes from straying towards the trees or gardens near our various quarters lest I start counting branches or flowers and get attached to my surroundings. But not this place. Despite the rent, the cruel landlord, the sagging roof, the fact that we lived every day under the lie of being Muslim, Ruby did not move us from Rehmat Nagar. For the first time, it started to feel like home.

I knew the reasons Ruby wanted to stay: Samuel and Tanya baji. Samuel lived and worked close by at a car dealership and Ruby was enjoying the new relationship, and Tanya baji had employed her as a maid.

Tanya baji was the daughter of a famous dead artist and the solemn widow of a journalist who was shot by unidentified gunmen ten years ago, over some controversial newspaper article. Now, she lived by herself in a decaying bungalow in the Upper Mall neighbourhood.

Whenever I mourned my polio-riddled arm or the friends I once again had to leave behind after yet another move, Ruby brought up the sad and lonely existence of her new mistress.

'Look at her. No father, husband, or mother. Living alone with a cat. Tanya Madam is living, breathing, isn't she? If she can do it, so can we.'

Yet Tanya baji was not the pitiable object Ruby painted her to be. In her, I saw a woman untethered. A woman who didn't need to beg for love. A woman in mourning, yes, but freer than anyone I knew.

She was in her forties, striking with thick, braided hair streaked with grey. She wore pastel chikankari shirts, cotton saris and Kolhapuri chappals. Her skin did not have vitiligo patches. Her arms and legs did not have polio. She was complete, and she glided through her 1930s colonial bungalow lined with paintings of women and horses, through wide, cool corridors with high ceilings and roshandans where pigeons had built nests.

To me, she was something out of the movies. Utterly surreal. Breathtaking.

When I met her for the first time, she was cleaning out a storeroom with the other housemaid, Shazia. There were boxes everywhere, piles of Christmas ornaments and a small artificial tree stashed away in the corner. In hushed tones, I asked Shazia if the mistress was Christian.

'She's Christian, Muslim, Hindu, everything,' Shazia replied, mockingly. 'She used to throw Holi parties for her friends in the garden. Christmas dinners every December and Eid functions twice a year. Though recent years have been quiet.'

Fewer parties. Fewer friends. Rarely any noise.

When the cleaning was done, as a thank-you, Tanya Baji opened a box and gave me a small, round ceramic ornament with a painting of the Virgin Mary.

'Here,' she smiled. 'I used to put it on the tree. My father brought it from Brazil.'

I placed it in the palm of my hand and studied the delicate piece in awe. A Virgin Mary adorned with a pale blue shawl bowed her head and stared gently at the infant Jesus cradled in her arms. A golden hue surrounded both the figures. I had never owned anything so spectacular.

'I don't like when she sleeps in the box,' Tanya baji said. 'Give her a home.'

Tanya baji had money, two cars, house help, an expensive-looking cat with long white fur and blue eyes called Kafka, a backup generator, and lots of spare time, which she often shared with me.

In the desert of Ruby's attention, Tanya baji's kindness felt like an oasis, and I eagerly drank up every last drop of warmth and consideration. Ruby's old mistresses had been scornful, plump housewives with drab appearances and rude tongues who never invited me inside the house. Tanya baji did not find my presence offensive. She did not mind if Ruby touched her flour, rice, lentils, or strawberries. She did not mind when Ruby wore a cross to work, or when Samuel came by on his loud motorbike to pick us up at night.

Tanya baji taught art classes to local children in her sprawling spring garden. To whittle the hours away while I waited for Ruby, I frolicked in the garden among the wild white roses, the yellow Tecomas, the bright orange zinnias and the purple petunias.

I found I could make myself happy with watercolours, poster paints and brushes even if I was surrounded by spoiled rich kids with Filipino nannies who wore T-shirts and tight jeans. These children spoke only in English.

But it was me, and me alone, whom Tanya baji enlisted to help with her errands. I proudly ran around the compound like a gleeful dove, fluttering here and there, working hard to make Tanya baji happy.

Wash this flat brush, please.

And so I did, under the garden hose.

Place this chart paper in that girl's trunk. Go grab the white paint from inside the house.

Oh, how it felt to be desired, to be needed, as if the class would shut down without me.

Every once in a while, a child would point at my coiled arm with fascination and disgust. 'What's wrong with you?'

'God installed a faulty one and we lost the receipt,' I'd reply.

Tanya baji had coached me in that answer.

'If people act shamelessly, you become shameless too. Remember that, Kaki, for no one in life will remind you.'

⁂

Although Ruby warned me to stay away from the neighbours in Rehmat Nagar, it was inevitable that I would make a friend. My loneliness demanded so.

My secret friend, Fatima, was the youngest daughter of Haji Miah Inaamullah Kareem. They lived two houses down from us. Haji Miah Inaamullah was not only our landlord but also a local cleric, a man of great influence, and someone deeply respected and feared among the Muslim families in the area. I had never seen a man like him. Abba had been a noisy man. A reckless man who lay here and there, unloved and unappreciated. But when Haji Miah Inaamullah walked through the streets, everyone greeted him with a salam, a free soda or a handshake. Young snickering boys stood up straight as he passed by. It was as if a king walked among us.

It was a Saturday afternoon when I met Fatima for the first time. I was buying corn from a vendor in the street, and she was playing cricket with a group of boys from the mohalla.

There was no school that day, and Ruby had gone to work in the bungalow alone.

Fatima approached me first, cricket bat in hand, with a familiar question. 'What's wrong with your arm?'

I took a big bite of corn and chewed in silence. Silence was necessary sometimes.

She answered her own question as she took an ear of corn from the old man with the donkey cart. 'It's polio, isn't it? I read about it in school. Why didn't your parents get you the drops?'

I looked at her feet in silence. Dusty, dirty toes snuck out from old pink Bata slippers. Embarrassed by the sight, I raised my gaze to her squinting face. I decided that I didn't like her hair. Her fringe was too short, as if a child had run scissors across her forehead. I also disliked the small scar on her eyebrow.

'Why didn't your parents get you the drops?'

'Why are you playing cricket in chappals?' I asked in return, not wanting to answer the question.

'Do you go to school?' I nodded.

'Where?'

'It's very far from here.' I pointed at an abstract distance, beyond the alley where we stood, beyond the colony mosque where Fatima's father recited the call for prayer five times a day. I did not want to mention my Catholic school.

'I go to the big one in the bazaar. Have you seen it? Muslim Girls' School ...'

I replied that I had when I hadn't.

'Do you want to play cricket?' She shoved the bat in my hand and gestured behind her to the group of boys standing in the narrow alleyway, to the Pepsi crate which they were using as wickets. The boys called out to Fatima, annoyed at the delay.

'No,' I shook my head, refusing to hold it.

The wooden bat fell between us, almost hitting her feet. 'Come on now.' She picked up the fallen instrument, held my good arm, and dragged me into the game. 'Come and field.'

She addressed the boys, and then me. 'She wants to play too. What's your name?'

'Kanwal.'

'Kanwal will play too,' she said decisively.

A small boy with long dark hair and shifty eyes muttered down to the floor, 'How will she play?'

'Better than you,' Fatima shouted back. She turned to me and smiled.

I smiled back at her loveliness, which showed itself to me in that moment.

'But we'll have to be quick, Kanwal, and finish the game before my father comes home. He doesn't like me playing outside with the boys. Even though they're all like my brothers.' Fatima leaned in close to whisper. 'Except for the Pathan boy. Do you see him?'

She pointed to a tall, light-skinned, light-eyed boy clutching a green tennis ball. He was the bowler. He was practising his delivery by hitting the crate over and over again.

'I'm going to marry him when I grow up,' she winked at me. 'Isn't Hannan handsome?'

He was. Handsome like those Hollywood actors Tanya baji watched in her movies. Creamy skin. Green eyes. Light hair. Normal hands.

When Ruby returned home that afternoon on Samuel's rickety motorbike, I was still playing in the alley with Fatima and the other children.

'Who's that aadmi?' Fatima pointed at Samuel, who was pushing his bike into our courtyard. 'Who's that man, Kanwal? I thought you said your father died.'

I did not reply. The men never stayed for long. I had become practiced in the art of forgetting.

⁂

Ruby, who had never given any man the upper hand, gave Samuel everything. Ruby, who had previously hankered for excitement, now cherished the stillness of a stable, simple life. Samuel was doing well at the car dealership. So well, in fact, that his boss, Rana Sahib, loaned him a new motorbike, payable in manageable installments. A performance-based bonus. Ruby said she would help Samuel with the monthly payments because we had become a family. If Rubina could help Abba, whom she did not even love, Ruby could help Samuel, whom she did. She liked Samuel's meekness, his devotion to her, his hard work, and now, his new, solid position as a supervisor at the car dealership. Before, he was a driver, but now he sat behind a clean counter and gave orders to other men.

'Do you remember Ghulam Rasool, Kaki?' Ruby asked me one day while we were in Tanya baji's kitchen. She was making broth and I was practising my English by trying to read headlines from a newspaper out loud. Tanya baji said that if I practiced reading different words in the newspaper, I would be able to speak fluently like the glamorous actors in fancy skirts we saw on television. I eavesdropped on her cellphone conversations too, hoping to pick up a few phrases. The way she spoke the language, so fluently, so elegantly, the unfamiliar words just rolled from her tongue like silk or melting chocolate. *Delightful ... wonderful ... Ridiculous ...*

'The man who gave you a mobile?' I asked Ruby. 'That Ghulam Rasool? The one who helped us move to Rehmat Nagar?'

'Yes, yes. What a bore that man was ... that Ghulam Rasool,' Ruby said. 'He works with Samuel at the car dealership, can you imagine? Ghulam takes orders from Samuel. Samuel is the boss. Ghulam saw me at the dealership when I went to meet Samuel last week. What a small, small world.'

She giggled the way Fatima did whenever she told me about Hannan.

'Samuel claims Ghulam Rasool is jealous of him. There must be something in me, no? Some magic that can spark such rivalry among men.' Her words were laced with excitement and pleasure. She was boasting. 'You only see such things in movies. And now I feel like I'm in a movie. Who knew?'

I folded the newspaper and set it aside to watch Ruby as she stirred the simmering broth with a wooden spoon.

'When I was younger, I dreamed of an exciting life,' she continued. 'But I got married.'

I looked at the pinkish-white stains on her brown hands, the shimmering red glass bangles which chimed softly as she moved her arm around and around. Her vitiligo, which had so often plagued her thoughts, seemed to trouble her no longer. Maybe being with a good man did that for a woman. Maybe being with a good man could make a person forget they had polio, too.

I could tell that Ruby's mind had taken flight. She was thinking about her new love. Endless horizons had opened up in her daydream. She was no Rubina, cautious and wary, afraid to overboil milk, fretting over my arm and my schooling. This was Ruby. And Ruby only thought about herself. She was a teenager in love. She wanted everything.

Sometimes I wondered if I reminded her too much of the past. Of Abba. We shared a nose. Did that remind her of him?

'Do you like my nose?' I asked.

'Hmm?' Ruby did not hear me, and I did not repeat myself. She turned off the flame and blew on the broth. I watched her put a little broth in a separate container for Samuel. She told me Tanya baji didn't mind sharing food. I watched quietly and found myself entangled in one of those bleak moments when I struggled to find my place in Ruby's universe. There I sat, unnoticed, anchored to the stool and yet very much adrift, floating across the kitchen tiles past stacks of potatoes and bananas, and there was Ruby, miles away from me, just out of reach.

⁂

That same night I asked Fatima if she thought I was beautiful. Fatima and I were sitting on my bed, cross-legged, flipping through old magazines, lingering over advertisements featuring tall, straight-haired women. Ruby had long since made her peace with my Muslim friend. As long as I didn't let slip our secret.

I asked her if my nose was too big or my arm too obvious. She did not understand why I brought them up. I pulled out Abba's old photo and showed it to Fatima. I trembled a little as I confronted that face after so long, those deep scowl lines on his forehead, the balding head and stained teeth. A flurry of memories, Rubina whimpering in the kitchen, cradled in my arms.

'Do you think I look like him?' I asked, shoving away the image.

'Did you think he was a handsome man, your father?' she asked.

I shook my head.

'Well, then,' she said, 'you do not look like him. You look like your mother.'

She smiled triumphantly, as though she had answered a trick question correctly.

'Very beautiful you are, Kaki,' Fatima remarked, licking her fingers and flipping a magazine. 'Just don't be any more beautiful, I don't want Hannan to fall for you instead of me.' Ruby walked by and gave us a suspicious look. She was in the midst of getting ready for Samuel to come pick her up. As soon as she was out of earshot, I closed the door to the room and scurried back to the bed, where Fatima was waiting with a piece of paper she had pulled from her bag.

'Now that we are friends, we share our secrets, right?'

I nodded solemnly. I had so few friends, I could not afford to risk losing one by saying the wrong thing. Fatima held up her hand and made me swear to God that I would not tell. I told her I would, though I did not swear to the same God as her.

Eagerly, she handed me the piece of paper.

'It's a love letter. For my Hannan. To show him how I feel.' I read it slowly, each word a tiny window into Fatima's heart, the deepest parts of her soul. I was being welcomed into her private thoughts, chosen to share in this secret. My toes grew warm with pleasure.

In showing me the letter, Fatima had opened the floodgates, and I felt compelled to offer a secret in return. I told her my mother did not believe in vaccines, which is why my arm was the way it was, and that sometimes I hated her for it. Fatima told me how her father beat her once for disobeying and how her older sister was betrothed to a cousin when she was just eleven. I told her of Ruby's boyfriends. Fatima told me that when she was eight, a shopkeeper crept his hand inside her trousers. I told her my father had not been a good man and often came home smelling strange, like something sharp and sour. It was alcohol. She said her father had another wife in another part of the city and her mother knew but kept silent. She was also quite certain he had more children. Maybe even another young daughter he loved more than her. Fatima's voice trembled as she made this final confession. She looked down at her lap, her shoulders quivering as her fingers played nervously with the corner of her kameez.

I slipped closer and wrapped my arms around her. I felt I should also tell her something big. Something to make her feel less alone, and so I did.

I told her we weren't Muslims.

'Really?' she asked, stunned by the admission.

I nodded in silence and told her that it was a secret. My eyes studied her face and waited for her to break my heart.

'Kasam khao.' She asked me to swear that I was a Christian.

And I swore. I went to my cupboard and took out the ceramic ornament from beneath a blanket. I showed it to her as a prized possession. She held the foreign object gingerly in her palms, slightly away from her body, as if it were a bomb that could go off with any sudden movement.

'What is it? Do you wear it? Is it a locket?'

I told her that it was a Christmas ornament Tanya baji gave to me.

'Is she a Christian?'

'No.'

'Then why did she have this?' I did not reply.

'Do you celebrate Christmas with the big decorated tree and gifts like they show in cartoons?'

'No,' I said. There had never been any money for a big tree and presents. 'We just go to the church service and make lunch at home.'

Silence hung between us. She rubbed her thumb over Mary's porcelain face. She bit her lip, thinking. I wanted to know what was running through her mind. I was dying to know.

'My father says you can't trust anyone who isn't a Muslim,' she said finally, her eyes wide. 'You didn't tell my father, did you? He would never allow you in this colony ...'

'But you can trust me,' I said, nerves clawing at my throat as I tried to reassure my friend that I was safe, touchable. 'And he doesn't know. We didn't tell. Don't worry.'

She deliberated in silence as I waited for her to rush out of my house, curse my name, denounce us as liars to the whole colony. I waited for the sacred, pious community to burst into flames, but instead my friend just said, 'It's okay.' As if my admission were nothing. As if it were as small as breaking a dish, or skipping a chore.

'But you'll help me, right?' she said, switching the subject. 'Will you help me deliver this love letter to Hannan? I'll keep your secret if you keep mine.'

We shook hands. I felt so accepted, so protected by her in that moment, that I swore I would.

⌘

A week later, Tanya baji and I were sitting in her garden during a power cut. Shazia was furious because someone kept taking the leftover lentils. She had to make the dish all over again.

'There was a bowl of it,' she said to Ruby. 'Now, I have to make it again in this hot weather. Who ate it?'

The backup generator had fried. It was getting darker. Birds were flying home. Mosquitoes buzzed in our ears and near our toes despite the Mospel lotion we rubbed into our skin. Dengue was on the rise.

Tanya baji sat in a bamboo chair with a flattened maroon cushion behind her back, a little sullen, and I sat in front of her on the grass. She asked me about my life, and I told her about Fatima from Rehmat Nagar. My Fatima from Rehmat Nagar.

'She's the cleric's daughter,' I said, fanning myself with a newspaper. 'She wants to run away to Murree or Kashmir with a boy she likes. You know her father is a maulvi, you know, a very strict man with a long beard and all.'

'And your friend doesn't mind befriending a Christian girl?'

I watched her tie her hair in a bun. Sweat glistened on her forehead and neck. Kafka lounged on the porch, watching birds fly home.

'Oh no, my Fatima does not,' I said. 'She doesn't care about such things at all.'

'How lovely, Kanwal,' Tanya baji said. '*Bohat acchi baat hai*. How lucky you are. See, usually children like those who their parents tell them they can like. Children unconsciously inherit their parents' tastes. When I was a child, my friends' parents did not allow them to come to my house. Do you know why?'

I picked at a fallen leaf, bending it down the vein, and shrugged.

'Because my father was an artist who painted half-dressed women sitting in the balcony of the red-light district.'

'Those kinds of women?' I asked in a low voice, abashed.

'Yes, the prostitutes in the Shahi Mohalla,' she said. 'We played loud music and had house parties. It was all very haram for my friends' parents. I had a very lonely childhood.'

I looked up at Tanya baji as she spoke. My beautiful Tanya baji with her red-bricked house and Rangoon creepers on the garden wall, surrounded by the fluttering Amaltas tree and the paintings of children she taught but didn't love.

⁂

Later at night, after the electricity came back on, Samuel picked me and Ruby up and drove us to get Chaman ice cream. Ruby told him that Tanya baji took lots of medicine to stay happy. She pouted and began reapplying lipstick where the ice cream had worn it away. A deep maroon. An expensive shade. The same shade that Tanya baji wore.

'There are medicines that can make you happy?' Samuel asked, raising his eyebrows. 'Why is the rest of the country not taking those medicines, then?'

Ruby laughed and wiped his mustache.

'What's wrong with her?' I asked as I lapped at my cone.

'She has depression,' Ruby said.

'What's that?'

'A disease for the rich,' Ruby said, waving her hand as if to dismiss the thought.

Samuel giggled. They were making fun of Tanya baji, and I did not like it.

⌘

I realized quickly that your past never truly leaves you. It slithers and snakes back in. The past cannot be packed up and tossed in garbage trucks, sealed and stored in a cardboard box in the basement. The memories bleed through. Climb up stairs and into bedrooms, darkening a person's dreams.

There were days I swore I could still smell Abba's perfume or hear his cough in the hallway. Feel his stare upon my back. Ruby had buried Rubina but she did not always stay dead.

Fragments of her, that sick life, still haunted my mother. I saw her tracing the pinkish-white patches on her hands and arms, lost in a reverie, as if the patches were a road map to the past. Abba had once told her that she was cursed. Samuel never said such things.

One night my mother woke up, engulfed in terror, screaming bloody murder. She was panicked, pathetic, helpless. She was Rubina once more. She wailed and howled as Samuel rocked her back to sleep like a little child. I watched from my twin bed on the opposite side of the room, peering at Rubina through the holes in my blanket. She kept asking my dead father to stop beating her.

With Samuel, my mother turned into many things—the child bride from Amrat Nagar, the insecure woman with a spreading vitiligo in Rehmat Nagar, the carefree woman who didn't care about the disease, the undying, undimming and haunted Rubina, the volatile, defensive Ruby, a woman madly in love.

⌘

Ruby was oiling Tanya baji's hair in the living room. Now and again the woman brought a lit cigarette to her lips and blew white-grey clouds into the high, cracking ceiling. She asked questions in between exhalations. 'Have your boyfriend and you ever thought of leaving this place?'

I watched the two from a crack in the kitchen door.

'We talk about it, baji, but as a joke,' Ruby replied. 'It isn't easy for people like us. Money, family nearby and whatnot.'

Tanya nodded in agreement. 'I feel the city is collapsing on me, burying me under its weight. The walls ... the walls of this house are closing in on me.' She placed her hands on her forehead.

Ruby, unmoved, continued massaging Tanya baji's scalp. 'I think about leaving all the time,' Tanya baji said. 'I feel my chapter here is over. I must begin again somewhere else. My friends are now mothers of teenagers. My brother has a good real estate business in America. And Imran, my Imran is dead. He is gone and I am here. Wallowing on this sofa, smoking into the ceiling. Year after year, it's the same. The melancholy.'

I yearned to comfort her, to burst from my hiding place and smooth the worry in her face, comfort her as I did Rubina, a lifetime ago. But I did not. I sensed Ruby would be angry. And so I remained hidden, a powerless bystander.

Ruby said something about entertaining more relatives and friends. Tanya baji said something about her body being on fire.

'I'm just so tired. This house is crowded with birds. Birds who hide in the ceilings and lay eggs. And then those baby birds fly away with their mothers and I'm left to clean up the straw and the shit and the shells.'

⁂

Ruby rejoiced in Samuel's successes, though not everyone did. People at work were jealous, he could tell. They whispered behind his back, let their envy bleed through every interaction, every false smile.

Samuel wondered if his Muslim employees did not like taking instruction from a Christian man. Ruby said it was human nature to be jealous.

I wondered if it was. I thought about Tanya baji's grace, about Ruby's beaming face when Samuel kissed her forehead, about Fatima and the boys who called to her in the streets when she went out. No one ever called me beautiful. The subtle pricks of envy I felt when I thought about all the other girls at school and on TV, with their perfect, smooth arms, thin noses and easy smiles. Their mothers and fathers who probably doted on them. In solitude, I cradled the ache in my heart.

⁂

As the embers of the scorching summer faded, October arrived with cool, rustling winds and sudden thunderstorms. After numerous rewrites, drafts, rounds of edits and last-minute additions, Fatima was finally ready for me to deliver her love letter to Hannan. This was a covert operation of the highest secrecy and I was honoured by her trust. Fatima relied on me. I could not let her down. She told me her father had once slapped her elder brother for arguing with a neighbour, so there was no telling what he would do if he discovered his daughter writing love letters to a boy. In the way that young girls dream too big and love too fiercely, I told her I would give my life to make sure the letter reached its destination safely. I believed that, too.

Fatima blessed the letter with a few verses from the Quran and handed it to me. I could tell that she was nervous. This one-sided infatuation terrified her. To a teenager, there is no worse fate than rejection.

I turned the folded letter over in my hands and considered the women in my life, and the men in theirs. Fatima and Hannan. Ruby and Samuel. Tanya and her long-dead husband. All three simmering in love. Yet what was love, I wondered, to make these women pine and yearn and cry and mourn and give their whole selves to another? To stop eating for days like Tanya baji or speak incessantly about nothing else like Fatima? It was a sinister thing, love. It was not warm. It was not sane. It was maddening. It ate them, and it starved me. My lack of it. Lingering on the edges. Asking to be loved. I turned the concept over in my head, trying to fit it within the contours of my brain.

One Sunday when Ruby and Samuel left to run errands, I took the neatly folded love letter and knocked at Hannan's door. I prayed to Jesus. I pictured the ceramic disk with Mother Mary in my head and prayed to her that he would be the one to open the door, and not his parents.

My prayers were answered.

I pushed the letter in his hands and rushed back home.

⁂

It seemed like the sun was swiftly setting on Ruby's love life. Times became desperate again.

There was bad news from Samuel's village. One of his sisters had contracted dengue and was languishing in a hospital bed. The medical bills alone ate up Samuel's entire pay cheque and half of his savings.

He could no longer pay for his motorbike, and Rana Sahib was not pleased. Ruby offered to borrow money from Tanya baji, but when she went to ask her for help, she was rebuffed. It seemed that Ruby had not yet paid off the previous loans she had received from Tanya baji, and the mistress explained that all things, even generosity, had limits.

⁂

Tanya baji started sleeping for long hours, smoking two packs of cigarettes a day, and scolding her maids and the gardener for not taking better care of the house. She stopped teaching art classes altogether.

A well-dressed, well-spoken man whom she called 'Mr Lawyer' or 'Lawyer Sahib' became a frequent visitor. He brought with him many stacks of paper. They talked for hours on end. I could not understand everything when they conversed in English, but I did pick up some words: 'home,' 'America,' 'pack up' and 'sell'.

'What's she doing?' I asked Shazia one day while the man visited.

'I think she wants to leave Pakistan,' she answered, removing seeds from a pomegranate to make juice for the guest.

I felt a knot in my stomach.

Shazia continued, 'I think she is tired of being here alone and wants to go to her family abroad. It makes sense. Family is family.'

'What will happen to the house?'

'Maybe she'll sell it to the government. It's a very old house. Or give it to a relative. Who knows what's going on in her mind nowadays? A cruel mistress is still better than an unstable one. At least the former is predictable.'

I had begun to shake violently, tears pooling in my eyes. Shazia asked me why I was so upset. She asked me why I cared so much.

'Do you think she'll stop if I tell her not to go?' I asked. She raised her eyebrows, surprised at my question. Ever honest, Shazia told me that no matter how much I begged or wept, I could not change another person's mind. I was not Tanya baji's blood. I was of little consequence. It was what it was.

'But don't you worry, Kaki,' she said. 'Your mother will find a new job. As will I. Masters come and go all the time.'

After the lawyer sahib left the drawing room, I asked Tanya baji if she would take me with her when she went away. I told her she could open an art school in America and I could be her assistant. She would need someone there to pack the paint and wash the brushes and shower Kafka and separate her summer clothes from winter. I could do everything.

She grinned, amused by my offer. 'And what about your mother? How can I take you from her?'

I told her that Ruby had Samuel. She would be fine without me.

'And what about your friend Fatima? Won't she be upset?'

'She will soon run away with Hannan to Murree,' I confided. I asked if she could make me her daughter. I had thought about this many times, and it seemed the best solution. I knew it was a strange request, but it was an earnest one.

'You have a mother, my child.' Tanya baji held my hand. 'But you'll always have a special place in my heart.'

That was not enough for me. I tried, desperately, but I could not peer into her heart. I could not see how many closets it had, and which shelf I occupied. Her consoling words were not enough. The bungalow was, though, and the sunny veranda with chipping paint, and the spring garden, and the snooty art class children with Filipino maids and Land Cruisers. They were all enough for me, and they should have been for her.

One night during an uproarious storm, Samuel came to our quarter after work, drenched in rain.

Water pounded down on the bedroom roof as he sat on the bed and dried himself with a towel. I peered out the window at his motorbike, which he had parked in the courtyard. There were scratches and dents all over the front of the vehicle. The headlight and mirrors were also broken.

'Rana Sahib said he would not pay me next month,' Samuel informed Ruby, despondent. 'I couldn't pay the installment on the bike. I had to send money for my sister instead. And look, I fell and broke the bike. Rana was fuming. Said I was useless. The other boys at the dealership think so too. They all hate me, I can tell.'

'But it's our bike,' Ruby said, examining a bruise on his arm, 'isn't it? I thought we had nearly paid it off.'

'No, we have months left to go. For now, it belongs to Rana, and I've damaged it. He wants full payment now.'

Samuel took out his mobile phone and tried to dial a number, but the rain had damaged the device. He hurled it angrily across the room, startling me with this sudden emotional outburst. The device hit a wall, shattering on impact.

I got up to retrieve the pieces on the floor.

As I squatted amidst the wreckage, running my hand through the remnants, the battery, the broken screen and attempted to reassemble the phone, my eyes fell on Ruby's face in the bedroom mirror. Mouth, downturned. Eyes shut. Breathing heavy.

'He's asking for sixty thousand ... He says I owe him the debt for the bike.' Samuel's head fell into his hands as he began to sob.

Ruby gave me a stern look, my cue to leave. I exited the room and pressed my body up against the outside wall, just beyond the door, so I could listen in.

'What will we do?' Samuel said. 'How can we afford to move now? Get a better place? How can I give you and the child a better life?'

I wondered if Samuel would leave Ruby. Return to his village. Abandon her as so many men had in the past. If Tanya baji would leave too. And Fatima. So many faces filtering in and out of my life. Ruby was already a stranger. Was I to be completely alone?

I knew Ruby's mind. I knew the surge of swirling emotions; this fortress of happiness she had sculpted in her imagination with Samuel was starting to crumble. The sturdy, stable walls and corridors were beginning to succumb to a new blow. We would have to move again. Begin all over again. A new man. A new neighbourhood, free of reminders.

Our lives had become an act of running away.

She spoke quickly, frantically, giving him ideas, promising Samuel that she would find a solution, asking him not to lose hope. She would find money: for his sister, for the motorbike, for his rent. How? When? Nothing mattered. She would.

Her words were muffled by the pelting rain.

⁂

The next morning, the alleys outside our quarter were littered with leaves, branches and dead insects. The roof of a nearby shop had fallen in the night and a young boy had died in the rubble. Trees lay felled in the streets.

Inside the bungalow, Tanya baji sat with her friends, discussing her upcoming move to a place called Los Angeles. Whether she would go at all. She was waiting for a sign, a divine intervention. Leaving Lahore was not a decision she could make on her own. Later that night I retrieved my ornament from its secret hiding place. In the dark I whispered to Jesus and Mother Mary and every other saint I could remember and pleaded, with all my heart, for a divine intervention of my own. If Tanya baji was waiting for a sign, let it come and convince her to stay in Lahore. With me. Forever. Cradling the ornament in my small, sweaty hands, I kissed the smooth object over and over again with such ferocity that I feared it might crack.

Ruby, meanwhile, was doing her own praying. At night she took me to church, far away from Rehmat Nagar. She was feverish with worry. She wanted us to pray. Rana Sahib kept asking for his money, and Samuel had none.

On the way home, as we snaked through the busy streets of the bazaar, we were stopped by a faith healer. His eyes roamed Ruby's spotted body, his crooked hand pointed to my shriveled arm. He said her skin was a curse from God, my deformity a punishment for the sins of the mother.

He called her a bad wife. An unfortunate woman. Enraged, Ruby unleashed a torrent of curses upon him. She took off both her slippers and threw them at the bald man. Then we hailed a rickshaw and went home.

Ruby was barefoot. I held her chappals as she cried. Loud, helpless sobs. A tearful monsoon. Love—being hopeless in love—was making a strong woman crumble.

This was only the second time I had ever seen Ruby cry.

I saw the ghost of Rubina flash across her face.

After a week, when Tanya baji thought I was out of earshot, she confronted Ruby in the kitchen. I was sitting on the steps outside, playing with Kafka. Tanya baji told her that twenty thousand rupees was missing from her cupboard. Shazia had seen the rustling, crisp notes in Ruby's hands. Ruby confronted the accusations, angry, and dared Tanya baji to search her clothes. Tanya baji said she would not. It was beneath her.

'I might not holler and raise a storm like other mistresses, Ruby,' she said. 'I treat my staff as family. Shazia, I have had for years. Saleem, the gardener, worked for my father too when he was alive. No one has ever let me down like you have.'

Ruby had said something in protest, something about there being a ghalat fehmi—a misunderstanding between them—maybe it was someone else who took the cash.

'But I'm not stupid.' Tanya baji did not yield. 'The missing food, bread, eggs, my makeup … I have never had a maid do this before. I hate to be on guard in my own house.'

Ruby dissented some more.

Tanya baji, unmoved, handed Ruby her wages and told her to stop coming to the bungalow.

'I don't mind if Kaki wants to come by,' she said. 'I have grown fond of the child.'

'If I'm not coming, my daughter isn't coming either,' Ruby said, defiantly.

I sat on the steps, hidden from both the women. I wanted to rush inside and ask my mother if it was true. I wanted to scream, to break down, to hit her. How could she cheat my Tanya baji like that? Break her heart like that?

At home, I told Ruby that if I wanted to go to the bungalow or sit in the garden or help Tanya baji with the art class or play with Kafka, I would. Nothing could stop me. I knew the way to the bungalow from anywhere in Lahore. I could be dropped blindfolded at the furthest corner of the city, and I would still be able to make my way back. It was home. I told Ruby that I was tired of moving houses and meeting new men who never lasted.

'The way she insulted and kicked your mother out, you still want to see that woman?' Ruby shouted.

'Did you steal?' I asked. 'Was she telling the truth? Did you steal? Did you steal?'

'I didn't steal,' Ruby replied softly. 'All those pills she takes, all those cigarettes she smokes, she's going mental.'

'You broke her heart,' I said. 'You think of nothing and no one but Samuel.'

'And you, too. I think and care for no one but the two of you.'

The piercing sound of Azaan from the neighbourhood mosque flooded the air.

'We're leaving this mohalla,' Ruby said suddenly. 'I feel unsafe. I can't sleep. This place is cursed ... And that Ghulam Rasool knows our secret. He helped us move. He knows we are Christian. And he's hell-bent on making sure Samuel loses his job. And your friend, Fatima, what did you tell her?'

She was erratic, utterly paranoid.

It was as if Haji Miah's call to prayer had awakened something inside of her. She was talking quickly now, as though trying to convince herself of the truth in her words.

'Samuel will look for a new job. We'll marry and we three will move somewhere else. Maybe even another city. And we'll be very happy.'

Ruby was ready to beat her wings and fly away again.

Ruby was ready to escape. 'We'll be very, very happy.'

I decided I would not follow.

'We'll finally be happy,' she muttered under her breath as she held my shoulders, looking for some acknowledgement in my eyes. But I gave her nothing. Instead, I let out a loud shriek. I told her I would not go anywhere with her. She could not make me. And if she tried, I would run away and she would never find me. I would run and run and run till my feet bled, but I would never come back to her.

I didn't want a new neighbourhood. I didn't want a new friend. I didn't want a new father. I didn't want to ride a motorbike. I didn't want to pack and unpack the bundles again. I didn't want to wander all my life.

I was tired. Of living in borrowed spaces like a nomad. Of surviving on scraps of love from transient relationships. Of trying to stitch together fleeting memories to make something of a life.

Ruby clamped my mouth shut with her hands. 'Stop talking. Stop talking. Stop talking. I am your mother. I know best.'

I wrestled my little body away from hers. I bit her hand.

She yelped like a wounded animal and quickly let me go. 'What kind of a mother are you? You didn't even give me polio drops. You should have buried me alive with Abba.' Tears swelled in my eyes. 'What am I to you, tell me? Who am I?'

She stammered but I continued, undeterred.

'I'm a liability, aren't I?' I cried. 'A dead weight you lug around while you dance away with these lovers. You shouldn't have been a mother. You shouldn't call yourself a mother. Jesus shouldn't have given you Kanwal. You go to your Samuel. You go to your Samuel!'

'Shut up, Kaki,' Ruby shouted. '*Batameez larki!*'

'You know what people think about you and all these men you see? Do you hear these whispers? They think you're a whore.'

Ruby did not respond with cruel words. Instead, she lifted her hand and struck my cheek with a sharp slap. My skin burned.

'Now, if you say that your mother is a terrible person, you can mean it.'

⁂

Ruby spent the night restless, roaming the courtyard, opening the front door at the faintest sound of a motorbike or rickshaw. While she paced from room to room, I curled under my blanket and seethed in my hatred for her. I wept uncontrollably. I hurled curses into my pillow. I pictured Tanya baji packing her bags, jetting off to America. I imagined Fatima's wedding to Hannan. I imagined an empty mohalla, and no one left to care for me. I wished I were Kafka, that rotten cat had it better.

I slept for hours on a tear-soaked pillow, and woke up to the sound of someone at the door. I closed my eyes again, expecting that it was just Samuel, coming for Ruby. Would she tell him, I wondered, about the stolen items from Tanya baji's house? About her plans to leave everything behind? To escape? About how I would not follow? I stirred from my sheets, listening for the sound of Ruby's squeals by the door. But instead I heard muted voices, muffled questions and footsteps towards my door. It was not Samuel, here for Ruby, but Fatima, here for me. I felt that my prayers had been answered. My friend, my lovely dearest friend, had come to speak to me, console me, rescue me.

'Why do you look so upset?' she asked, walking into the bedroom. There was no trace of warmth in her voice.

I sat up. My lips quivered and I rubbed my swollen eyes.

Before I could answer, she spoke again.

'Did you tell Hannan the letter was from me?' Her coarse tone frightened me. She had never spoken to me like that before.

'You didn't, did you?

'Didn't you sign the letter?' I asked, disoriented, pulling the bedcovers off. 'Didn't you write your name?'

'Why would I sign my name?' she said. 'Do you want me to get caught? But now he thinks the letter is from you. My brother told me that Hannan asked about you ... fondly ... He asked if you might come to our next cricket game. He says he likes you too.'

I struggled to find words. She unleashed a tempest of emotions. Her words were scathing, unfiltered. I got on my feet and approached her. I pleaded for her to listen. She did not. Her face contorted with rage. Her monologue pierced the air as she held back tears.

'I don't understand,' I said, rattled. 'I don't understand what you're saying ...'

'Stop playing stupid.'

'I swear on Jesus.'

'Father says Christian women have loose characters,' she spat. 'I see now that he was right.'

I was crushed. My heart shattered. Fatima asked me if I wanted him, if I loved him, if he loved me back, if I loved him as much as she loved him, if I had betrayed her, sabotaged her, if I would steal him from her. Though who was I, she asked, to think he would choose me over her? Was I Katrina Kaif? Was I Aishwarya Rai? I was a deformed, scrawny, poor little thing. 'Stop talking,' I pleaded. 'You're scaring me. Please stop.' She was breathing heavily. Anger clouded her face. Yet even with my broken heart, I still tried to comfort her, persuade her that she was mistaken. I was on my knees, holding her hand, begging.

'My father was right,' she kept sobbing, shaking her head. 'You can't befriend a Christian. Christians are not loyal. You are different from us.'

She went to the cupboard and took out my ornament. 'Leave Rehmat Nagar, leave my Hannan,' she said, 'or I'll tell my father your secret.'

When I saw the orb in her hands, I became enraged. I snatched it from her.

'You're horrid,' I said. 'I hope you're never happy. I hope Hannan marries a cousin. I hope you fail your exams and rot in hell. Muslim hell.'

She said nothing in reply. She cleaned her snot with her dupatta and dashed for the door.

I did not follow her. I remained where I was. I remained how I was. Dishevelled. Disillusioned.

There was a feeble, brittle sound. I looked down and saw the ornament, snapped in my hands. In my anger, I had clutched the fragile thing too tightly. Broken it into two clean slices.

Jesus separated from Mary.

⁂

Night fell and still Samuel had not arrived. By then, Ruby had started to worry. Something was wrong, she said. She could feel it in her guts, in her veins, in her heart, in her bones. Samuel had become a part of her, of her body, her being. She could feel when something was amiss. It was as if someone had severed her leg and she could not find the missing limb.

'Maybe he just left,' I said, looking up at her nonchalantly from my bed.

My mind was haunted by Tanya baji and Fatima's silence, and now by Ruby's growing madness.

'That's not possible.'

I reminded her of the other men who had betrayed her even when she swore they would not. There was the man who was afraid of her vitiligo, the other who did not like that she came burdened with a daughter. Others left for no reason at all.

Ruby mumbled something to herself, looked up at Jesus, and said a prayer. She peeked out at the alley as if expecting Samuel to leap out and embrace her in surprise. I realized how much I pitied women in love. How messy they were. How wretched. All of them. Including me.

The women in the Bollywood movies I watched with Fatima. Soaking and singing in the rain like lunatics, making themselves sick in chiffon saris as they danced in snow-capped mountains, pining for a man's attention. The wretched characters in the books Tanya baji read. She told me about Ophelia, Juliet, Sassi, Anarkali. Curse them all. Dying uselessly for a man's love. Ruby, like a teenager in love, swayed by pretty gifts and free rickshaw rides. And me.

The most wretched of them all. Grief-stricken and alone. A discarded thing.

Eventually, Ruby calmed down enough to sit and rest her head on a pillow. I pulled out the rolled-up Jesus Christ calendar from the cupboard and placed Christ between us on the bed. She kept her hand on his pale face as I shushed her, pacified her.

Through the slit in the curtains, a beam of yellow streetlight sliced the darkness in the bedroom.

Ruby looked straight at me. Her face was sallow and her eyes swollen from the weeping. I didn't know if I could call her Ruby at that moment. That confidence, that fire, that spontaneity had vanished. It seemed like all the Rubinas, the Rubys, the Ammas had melted away, and she had become one complete, miserable child. There was no woman anymore.

'You're right,' I said. 'I think we should move. There's nothing here for us.'

My mother nodded and closed her eyes.

I lulled her to sleep with consoling thoughts. *Samuel was a good man, but good men sometimes make mistakes. If he did leave, I would be there to help her through the mess. She would love me more. I would love her more.*

I wanted that moment to last forever. Our fingers interlocked. Frozen together. I had my mother.

'Get me something to eat,' she said, fatigued. She reached into her bra and pulled out a crumpled wad of money.

I took two hundred rupees.

'Maybe I dreamt of him,' she whispered, drifting off.

'Maybe I dreamt of a time when Fatima was my friend,' I said.

'Maybe Samuel never existed,' she said.

'Maybe I dreamt of the bungalow and the water paints, and the pigeons, and Kafka, and Tanya.'

'Maybe it has always been just us,' she muttered, her last words before she fell asleep.

Alone and hungry, I left the quarter to go buy groceries for our empty kitchen. Ingredients to make my mother's favourite potato curry. I would show her, starting now, that I could be just as useful as Samuel. Just as comforting. She only had me. I had only her.

I went to a tandoor nearby to get roti. I walked past the boys playing cricket with makeshift wickets. Fatima was not there. One of them, a small, frail thing, raised his hand to stop the game and beckoned the rest over. They were watching some loud video on his cell phone. I peeled off a few posters on my way out of the mohalla. The wicked politician promising great change. The lying travel agent promising a better life abroad. I scrunched the papers in my hand and tossed them into the rubble.

Better is a lie, I thought. *This is it. This is life.*

As I waited for the shopkeeper to make my change, a beggar with an arm ugly and coiled like mine approached to ask for money. He extended his trembling hand, pleading. I quietly handed him the fifty rupees I was left with.

'May Allah give you everything your heart desires,' he prayed.

'Will he?' I mumbled.

The shopkeeper wrapped my rotis in a cocoon of old newspaper and asked me if I had heard the news about the man on fire. Everyone was talking about it. I said I had not. I do not know why, but I felt a cold shiver trace down my back.

'You haven't?' He was shocked. 'Do you have a mobile? Do you have 4G? They set a man on fire ...'

'On fire?' I asked softly.

'Fire,' he continued. 'Just like that, a man turned to ash.' Before he explained, two customers demanded his attention. He disappeared inside the crammed shop.

An auntie from the mohalla sitting on the steps outside her quarter asked me about it as I returned home. I had never spoken to her before but was curious for news, curious enough to talk to a stranger. She said a raging mob had burnt a Christian man in an auto shop. They doused him in petrol and set him on fire.

'A whole walking, talking, living human being,' she said. 'Now he is nothing but ash.'

'Why?'

'The workers are saying he insulted Islam. Apparently he was stealing motorbikes, too.'

My stomach churned. I found it hard to breathe. 'But did he?' I asked in a whisper. The chill grew.

She shrugged, 'Who knows? Who knows what happened?' She summoned another man walking by on the street.

Like me, he stopped and came over to chat, though he had a mobile phone and was able to show us the video.

It was making headlines. Throngs of people taking photos in front of a body being stoned as it burned. The body did not move. It was bloody. Perhaps there was still a heartbeat. Yet people smiled and pouted and posed triumphantly as they took pictures.

Hundreds of people circled a burning body. You couldn't see much, just black ash and fire. You couldn't hear much, just the indistinguishable roar of the crowd. It was hard to imagine that there was a fully formed human somewhere in there. Underneath that petrol. Underneath that fire. Underneath those stomping feet. In that ash. Someone with a family back in the village. Someone with a grieving lover, burdened with fears of the future, who had just fallen asleep.

Acknowledgements

Before I move on to the remarkable guides and faithful, tireless companions who helped shape this book, can I pause to honour a library desk and a flickering lamp? Can I offer gratitude to the tree I watched fall, bloom, wither and rise again from my apartment window in Morgantown—a silent witness to my displacement? And what about the lingering scent of my late grandmother's dupatta—can it, too, be cherished like a melancholic, forgotten song and find a place here?

As these fragments of memories weave themselves into the fabric of these pages, so I, too, acknowledge the people who have been crucial in bringing this book to life.

To my agents, Lily Dolin and Lucy Luck, who believed in my voice from the very first submission to the final, and understood every heartbeat beneath a line, and guided me as this book found its balance, rhythm and place in this world. To Dharini Bhaskar, my editor at HarperCollins India, whose faith in both this book and in me has been a steady, nurturing light. It means much that the book now travels across the subcontinent, where its journey feels complete.

For my biggest champion at West Virginia University, Glenn Taylor, for embracing my beloved city, Lahore, without ever needing to kiss the land, and always believing my work had space in the literary wilderness. A big thank you to the Department of English at West Virginia University for granting me the privilege of a teaching position and for empowering me both as a student and teacher during my time there.

To Mahwish, my first call for every big news, every moment of doubt and every victory. And foremost, my precious Nat, who I met in the hallways during my MFA years and who has always been my first reader, guiding me through all things American. You've listened to my ramblings and helped me decode complexities. Thank you for all the math we did over 3 a.m. calls—the I-79 routes, animal imagery, figuring out how many inches of snow is actually too much snow, and whether the red parka was too much of a statement for a story. You have truly been my best translator of both language and life.

Lastly, I would like to express my heartfelt gratitude to *American Literary Review*, The Punch (India), *Salamander*, *The Malahat Review*, and *Greensboro Review* for first publishing a few of these stories and providing a home.

About the Author

Kanza Javed holds an MPhil from Kinnaird College for Women and an MFA in fiction from West Virginia University, where she received the Rebecca Mason Perry Prize. She is the winner of the Reynolds Price Prize for Fiction and has been a finalist for the New Millennium Writing Award, the *Salamander* Short Fiction Contest, and the Robert Watson Literary Prize.

Her debut novel, *Ashes, Wine and Dust* was shortlisted for the Tibor Jones South Asia Prize. Javed's short fiction has appeared in *American Literary Review*, The Punch Magazine, *Salamander*, *Greensboro Review*, *Narrating Pakistan* and *The Malahat Review*. Most recently, her work was featured in *In the New Century: An Anthology of Pakistani Literature*, edited by Muneeza Shamsie.

HarperCollins *Publishers* India

At HarperCollins India, we believe in telling the best stories and finding the widest readership for our books in every format possible. We started publishing in 1992; a great deal has changed since then, but what has remained constant is the passion with which our authors write their books, the love with which readers receive them, and the sheer joy and excitement that we as publishers feel in being a part of the publishing process.

Over the years, we've had the pleasure of publishing some of the finest writing from the subcontinent and around the world, including several award-winning titles and some of the biggest bestsellers in India's publishing history. But nothing has meant more to us than the fact that millions of people have read the books we published, and that somewhere, a book of ours might have made a difference.

As we look to the future, we go back to that one word—a word which has been a driving force for us all these years.

Read.